ISBN: 9798454782962

Contents

Besties share everythang!

A Toxic Love Story

Sparkle Riley

Dedication

Best Friends share everythang. They really do. Crazy stuff like cutting up and turning out. Covering up their sneaky links together. The playful roasting mixing with a little harmless backstabbing. The two faced times when y'all wasn't on the best of terms. That ride or die was it and you ain't never expect her to do you dirty. The late-night drivebys around his crib like a crazy chick. I mean y'all go way back to playing with plastic barbie dolls, jump rope and hula hooping. I mean y'all was tight, tight once upon a time. That was until one of y'all got a man who ain't got no availble brothers or cousins. At least a homeboy or somebody for the clique, right. Oh, it's about to go now. The jealousy and the hating on you ain't no joke. Y'all might as well through y'alls whole friendship in the trash. If the trust is broken and your bestie is a thot, too. It might even be both of them on the low. What you going to do? For these three besties, they going to do what they got to do for theirs by all costs. It's about to be lit in the streets of Baltimore City.

If you got that one friend that ain't carrying you greasy. You good, Sis! Y'alls friendship made it. Heck, dedicate to them for real because finding and trusting somebody, anybody is off the chains. Be careful and don't hook up with these three, Shabria, Neicy or Trina. Sometimes you got to cut people loose, y'all. Value and love the good friends you got. Being cool like that is priceless. Do I have any regrets? Not really just time lost and I can't get that back or go back in time. The good news is that eventually everyone will get past the betrayal at some point. You got to move on and not waste time on the you know who or who's. I mean seriously, Sis. This can be you, too. Those days,

months and years went by fast to get to this point. *Unbothered*! The idea for "Besties Share Everythang" came about because I know somebody somewhere is going through the same thing. I got to point that out and keep it 100! That all advice isn't good advice. Can't nobody say anything if they have never walked in your shoes before. As far as the trust thing, always keep your eyes and ears open. If it's yours, keep it close. If it is snatched away from you, then uh. Y'all already know what time it is. I wrote this fictional love story solely out of creativity. Who doesn't like a toxic love story these days? I can't lie but they do be lit. Once you experience that type of toxic, urban love, most of us can't go back to the boring flowers and candy type of love. Besties share everythang is just that, too! It's an Urban Romance that's on a whole other level. It's about testing your limits and asking how much you will or will not accept in love. There has to be a point where you must draw the line for your own peace and sanity. You can know somebody your whole life and still not know them at all for real. Like my main character, Shabria Reid on the cover. Our girl represents a lot of people, especially single mothers. Some of us have been there and done that. Trying to date and hook-up while their kids are sleep in the house. Dating with any kind of baggage is going to be hard. You will always have to compromise, sacrifice and adjust to being in a new relationship. Balancing a single parent home is difficult financially, emotionally and physically. Especially, if the guy doesn't have kids like my dude, Ricoe in this here book. A man like that with no olife's demands or responsibilities.

Finding a babysitter for one or just having extra free time on your hands. Time management is an obstacle while juggling multiple tasks at one time. Y'all know how that is! Eventually,

we can do it for the right person when they walk into our lives. They still got to be willing to support, uplift and inspire us. It gets messy for my character, Shabria real quick though. Imagine, if you got a jealous best friend who's a thot, y'all know it's over right! Y'alls respect and friendship is going in the dumpster. Might as well throw the whole friendship in the trash. Especially, when your home girl suggests sharing *your man* like you do everything else. To say that he gonna cheat anyway so it might as well be her, is crazy, crazy. Even if her new man, Ricoe was still for the streets that should have never crossed her best friend's Neicy's mind for real. Like who, does that? Even if Shabria considered it, can she trust that her home girl, Neicy would be okay in the side chick place forever though? Of course, her new man is all for it. Shabria is in love and it is toxic as hell. Both of them is willing to do whatever to make their new love last. But how much is too much? Are you willing to risk it all for love though? As a woman, what are you willing to sacrifice just to please your man? If he is doing everything right, should getting some on the side even matter for real? As a single man without a wedding band on, should you be completely single? Are you required to play the stepdaddy role? Well, that's what Shabria and her new man has to decide, y'all! Either way, Sis got problems. She figured I'm damned if I do and I'll be dammed if I don't? Shabria figures if he is still for the streets.......

Introduction

This right here is for my ladies. Y'all guys, too. I got to say it loud for my people in the back, you feel me. Who hasn't been dragged by a show of hands? Everybody and they mama is out here searching for the perfect Mr. or Mrs. Right. We know daggone well that such a person may not exist, right? But we still fantasize about them and make them a perfectionist. That's only in our eyes though. We put that man or woman so high on a pedestal that they just can't do no wrong, right. Take these chatlines and Facebook dating apps. It's free so you can't go wrong. Who hasn't tried really by a show of hands? I get it because they do be tempting! Sure, but we all know that anybody can make a fake profile with filtered pics. If they can't show face, then what's the point of us wasting time by facetiming and texting. Keeping it 100, it's a waste of time for most of us. Who wants to be catfished in 2022? You can be anybody you want to behind that screen! Who knows what is or isn't true these days? Fake statuses, hurt feelings and gaslighting is for the birds, for real. I say throw the whole dating pool in the trash. If it ain't toxic, I don't want it. I heard that toxic luv be lit. The kind that gets you twisted up in your own lies. When you stay doing uncoordinated cartwheels, bending over backwards and flipping out over that love. You yank on your significant other like a rubber band type of love. The more you pull on it, the further they get away type of love.

It will have you singing and smiling at the time type of love. Get bit instead of a hickey thing! The red flags is all good. The love that makes you do wrong when it feels so right. Chase you with a fly smacker and have hot grits in a pan thrown at you. That was just how Shabria and Ricoe was kicking it, too. When you get all delusional and blame yourself for them cutting up.

Chopping it up today has a whole new meaning for lovers of today. For Shabria Reid, the streets are talking but she's not trying to hear that. The East Baltimore Project's wasn't ready for all that though. There is nothing like that first taste of raw, unfiltered love, y'all. Shabria and most of us want it. I do. I did and is still addicted to it. Shabria is just tied! There is nothing worse than being bitter, penniless and down in the gutter. You get tied of the corner thugs still living with they mama. Lil' Day-day with his five baby mama's and ten bad ass kids. The Black Tony's, Lil' Rickie's and Slim Dante's ain't making the cut no more for our girl. Shabria is sick of greasy chicken boxes and bootleg DVDs on they mama couch. That mess is played out. Shabria wanted to go the movies out Arundel Mills or White Marsh to switch it up a little. Shabria wanted that real popcorn with extra butter. Let her sit back in the reclining chairs with her feet up type of date for a change. With her baby daddy incarcerated, our girl just felt alone and lonely for real. Shabria wanted to know where the working brutha's be at? The one's that like to take a sista out the hood for that county lobster, aged old wine and have the waiter hook you up with fancy floss packs. Shabria desired that type of thug who opened doors occasionally but still might leave your tail at the corner when he got mad. He have you out there catching hacks and the number five bus in a heartbeat type of thug. A gray pair of pants wearing thug that gave you his checkbook periodically. He who is the romantic type is definitely a keeper. Who doesn't want a thug who frequently buys us flowers after a night of cheating and running the streets. He loves to date you but will stand you up at Golden Coral in a heartbeat type of love. That Ricoe Jones off the chatline was just that, too. Street smart, foul and a lil' intelligent.

Dangerous, a lil' ruff but hella fun. Ricoe Jones was all that, ladies! Her ideal man got to be a lil' bit single but not too much drama. If he is hiding a wedding ring though then it becomes a messier love thing. Nobody will ever know because her new man stayed to himself all the time. Shabria ain't want him in no situationships or entanglements though. Who does for real? Let's just say your girl hit the lotto when Ricoe Jones a.k.a Black King rode in slinging 12 inches. Woo child, he said all the right things to get them drawls on the first date. The wooing and courting ain't never stop! Rose petals in the tub, shopping sprees and a new whip. Hello!

That man left his cellphone on and wasn't no sneaky calls or links popping up on his screen, ladies. No chicks or thots was ever sliding in his dm's. The type of man that checked in like that. "Bae, this is where I be and this is what I'm doing, a'ight," toxic lover type. Ricoe didn't have time to cheat because he stayed up under her like gravy smothered over porkchops love, y'all. Who don't want that?

It was all good until his ass got real sneaky and slick mouthed. Lying about lil' dumb shit. Possibly even messing around with her best friend, Neicy with the phat ass. Leave it up to Ricoe and she was the one that was delusional and too insecure. A homeless man was even checking for her man. The

streets is calling him Remy but he says his name is Ricoe! Like they say though, a woman's intuition ain't never lie though. Shabria was trying to figure out if she's losing her mind, her man or both? Should she care or just get that head, bread and leave? Cause she damn sure wanted to open her own salon! They both toxic as hell and chop it up like two crazy ass people all day long. That old saying goes that after ninety days, the love things gets stale, boring and ran over.

Shabria been with her Bae, sixty days and she already was shaking her head. Who is this man for real? My lover, provider and future step-daddy to my babies? Something ain't right and Shabria could feel it! Her man was too good to be true. What she going to do about it is the problem? Her and her babies live in a tiny apartment in the East Baltimore Projects as it is. Nobody wanted to live paycheck to paycheck when you can have a man like Ricoe Jones! Look if you ain't on section eight or qualify for food stamps what you going to do. Your kids is fed and, on the surface, you got you a working man. Where he works, nobody knows. Sometimes a baby muva got to weigh out her options at the end of the day. He got money and Ricoe is paying all her bills. He is sexy and chocolate too. Maybe he's an introvert because of his tragic past. At least that's what he said....

Chapter One: The Barbeque

It had to be the hottest day of June to be chopping it up in the hood. There's nothing like a BBQ in the ghetto! Especially an illegal one on somebody else's property, lol. Shabria and Ricoe knew that shit was dead wrong and still had it lit anyway. That was the thing about them low-income apartment buildings. Y'all ain't have no balcony, air conditioning or nothing. Them cheap box fans wasn't cutting it. It was too damn hot to breathe in Baltimore City that day. The index reached 106 degrees in that joint. Sweating bullets and wearing sticky clothes like that was torture. Not having two pennies to rub together made it worse. It was the middle of the month and the Cherry Lane Apartment tenants ain't have a pot to piss it in. Their social service and child support checks was running out like a track star. Can't nobody sell and keep food stamps like that as it is. It be just enough food to get by for real. Them struggle meals ain't no joke. Ain't but so much oodles of noodles and Vienna sausages one can take. Them nasty ass can ones at that. At least the name brand would have helped out a lil' bit!

Now take, the project Black King who was all in love and shit. He had to do the most to impress his new boo thing, Shabria that particular day. Their relationship was still new like a newborn. They were in the ain't we so precious stage. The early days of admiration, adoration and the bubbly, cuddly phase. Like that

sweet baby powder. You got to sprinkle sweet happiness to keep that love fresh everywhere that counts. Today, he was showing his girl's hood some love big time. He had a couple of dolla's so it was no thang to see his girl cheesing like a hyena.

"Shabria, I got to hand it to you girl. Me and Trina ain't think y'alls love thing would have lasted this long for real. It was just the other day when you was down in the gutter under you know who. Your man over there firing up the grill by himself and shit with his sexy, chocolate ass! Look at him looking like, oh I know I'm the shit over there. Y'all must be doing a'ight, Sis! Them babies you got rocking new Jordans and shit. Must be nice considering all your ass went through. I speak for all the single ladies in this hood, word! We want to know if his ass got a brother, uncle, father, muva or something. I'll even holla at his sista if she is as fine as he is!" said Neicy as she swallowed down her second cup of Hennessey. That Neicy loved some Henny now. All she needed was some liquor and another woman's man to be off the chain.

Shabria was blushing because her man was doing the damn thing! It was all his decision too. He was like Bae, "Let's go to the market to pick up a few things." Shabria thought ain't nothing wrong with that. But being in love had him doing the most too. Her man did more than just pick up some stuff. Ricoe done went and bought all Giant's shit. He was snatching all the food off the shelves and the freezer section. Ricoe kept cheesing while piling their cart up like a pyramid and shit. After a while, she did too. Her man insisted that she do the same, so she did just that. She personally would have preferred the beauty hair store herself. You can never stack up on enough grease, hair glue and spritz to save yo' life. Shabria didn't know what was going on until

they got to Walmart. His ass was showing off, a'ight. He bought out the whole patio section like what. A big ass family reunion type of grill, y'all. Them picnic canopies and umbrella tables and chairs.

When her man told her what was up, she straight kerked out on his ass right in the aisle. Other customers were shaking their heads and calling them young and ghetto. They kept right on arguing and cussing and didn't pay them people no mind. Shabria was straight out against what her man was saying because it violated her lease. Cookouts weren't allowed and violators faced eviction. But you know her Bae. Mr. Suave, smooth talker can get what he want when he wants it. *He damn sure got them drawls on the first date*, laughed Shabria to herself.

Ricoe's explanation was you got to take risks sometimes. Life was too short to always play by the rules. He danced in fire and walked into danger. Ricoe often joked that he would go through fire to make her his wifey and crazy shit like that. He always said, "I ain't never scared of shit, Shabria." But that was her man tastefully foul with a f*ck*d up way of thinking and Shabria loved that shit.

"Girl, I don't know what my man got for real. A'int that some crazy shit. He don't mention nobody and I ain't stupid enough to ask him. If he want me to know, he'll tell me. I ain't trying to mess our shit up. Know what I mean? A man like Ricoe is too hard to come by, a'ight. I finally can get rid of my rose thing, ladies! Oops, did I say that nasty sh*t out loud? My bad ladies," laughed Shabria and Neicy. Trina's ass ain't said a word since the cookout started. *Oh well, f*ck that sh*t cause I don't have time for it today*, thought Shabria.

Shabria looked at her homegirls, Neicy and Trina and shook

her head. That Neicy was a piece of artwork. Ghetto, ratchet and thottish at its best. Neicy did whatever and whoever she wanted. Shabria often wondered what turned her girl out like that. Neicy took hide and seek to a whole new level. While the other little girls was hiding, she was doing the nasty. Her little nasty self was giving blow-jobs to all the little boys and letting them do whatever. At twenty-seven, Neicy was still out there hoeing in the Baltimore Streets. With her long, cheap ass weaves and fake spider eyelashes on. In all that heat, Shabria couldn't believe that all that corpse makeup ain't melt as hot as it was. To this day, Neicy still let anybody hit for forty dollas or even two-dollas if the man looked good. It still wasn't nothing in Neicy's upbringing to f*ck her up like that. Neicy was just pitiful and sad. Such a pretty girl with pretty natural hair. She ain't even need makeup and skimpy clothes to get a man's attention. Shabria was tied of talking to that hoe for real. At the end of the day, Neicy was a grown ass woman. As long as she ain't mess with hers, they asses was good. If her *ss want to be a pornstar for free that's on her. To date, her *ss ain't have shit to show for it. Shabria was bopping her head to the summer latest and just chilling for real. A couple of shots had her real nice. Shabria was contemplating on some hookah for real. She ain't never really f*ck with weed because it be laced with other shit.

Shabria looked over at her other homegirl, Trina for a second. Trina with the stank attitude and stank face. Shabria believed the b*tch was low-key jealous of her because she was a pretty, red-bone. Trina's skin tone was coal black but she was so freaking stunning to her. Her and Trina had been friends for damn near twenty some years and she felt like she still ain't no sis like that. That Trina was too damn quiet if you asked her.

Trina ain't going to say shit to yo' *ss. Trina was that one friend who just listened to whatever you had to say. It was like talking to a blank wall and shit.

That's why they got along so well. Nobody in the projects knew what made sis tick and that shit was crazy for real. Trina ain't never cry, smile or nothing.

Shabria made it her business not to spill no tea around her weird ass though. Even Trina's *ss couldn't be trusted around her new, bae either. Shabria wasn't nobody's fool now. These so called chicks can be low-key thotiannas in a minute. Them low-down jealous hoes who be wanting your man behind your back and sh*t. Trina's ass was too pretty to be crazy like that for real. Shabria and Neicy definitely ain't want to get old girl pissed! Neicy shot Shabria a look to peep Trina.

"Trina, is you enjoying yourself over there? You ain't eat or drink nothing since you got here, Sis. All this food and liquor, Trina. Did I mention free, Sis?" said Shabria with a sincere smile. What she wasn't about to do was pacify her a*s all day though. It was a m*therf*cking ghetto BBQ in the projects, ain't nobody had time for that hot a*s mess right there. She either eat or drink the sh*t or not. That * was on her.

"I'm good Bria. Thanks for asking though. I'm surprised the police ain't roll-up on your shit. We not supposed to be out here on these people property like that. It ain't like we ain't have no other options and sh*t. At Druid Hill Park, it's only three-dollas to swim and the city allows you to BBQ out there," said Trina all crazy like. Even simple acting, Trina black ass was still pretty as shit. Trina could have been a runway model with her striking features and exotic looks. Trina had a cute baby face, perfect figure and some pretty a*s white teeth on her. Trina was the pret-

tiest one out the three of them. Trina lived in the projects with both her parents, unlike her and Neicy. Her parents worked and had a couple of dolla's. Why they stayed in the housing projects was beyond her. Her mother was a nurse and her daddy was an electrician. So, it was like what the fuck Trina?

Who'd want to live in the ghetto with the section eight and social service tenants by choice? I mean my girl's peeps was decent. They was just good around the way people and shit. *Just weirdos I guess,* thought Shabria. Anyway, the b*tch was acting uppity and stale and ain't nobody like that sh*t.

Shabria just ignored the silly hoe. Today was all about her and the new man in her life. Her man, Ricoe Jones was a God send for real. Ricoe just happened to show up at the right time and place. Shabria had been praying for a man like that for a long a*s time. The odds of snagging a Ricoe Jones type of brother was slim to nothing. Just a little bit more and she would have had to apply for social services and section eight her damn self. Her mother had been low-key hating ever since her man came into her life for real. The struggles for a single baby mama with kids is f*cking real. Her mama tried to act like she ain't know how it was in them streets. Shabria was tied of working two low, minimum wage jobs to prove a point to her old a*s self all the time. It's been a many of times where she damn near had to sell c**chie to put food on her table for her babies. Sis was tied of all that struggle shit.

Being a single muva ain't never been no curse but when shit hit the fan that's a different story. Her mama, Tawanda been bad mouthing her man ever since her man been in the picture for real. Tawanda stayed talking sh*t about her new man and for no good reason really. All Bria heard was her man ain't worth shit.

*"His black a*s is sneaky as shit. Where his a*s work at? He gots to be a drug dealer, a gang banger or a convict, Bria. All money ain't good money, Shabria. Believe that Bria."* She couldn't get her mama's nagging voice out her head for nothing. Her mama's words was sticking to her hair like some old bonding glue for real.

Shabria thought it had to be jealously or why else would her own mama show out like that? Her wrinkled, gray haired self was just hurt and bitter and on her own shit. Every man out there was no good, cheating a*s, lying a*s dog to her. Tawanda ain't believe into taking accountability for her part in it. *Sh*t, it takes two to tangle*, thought Shabria. All men ain't sh*t was her Mother's day to day motto. Shabria looked at it like this. What did her man have to do with her stupid ass life choices and sh*t? Like what the f*ck, Ma for real?Her dumb a*s literally chose to stay with those lying, cheating fools all that time, right! So, how is it always the man's fault and sh*t. All I know is that she better than me. Shabria wanted to know what Tawanda expected that man to do. I mean all the red flags was all up in her face. It had to be her mama's low self-esteem or something. A light bulb should have come on a long damn time ago. When did settling and desperation ever keep a man that ain't want to be kept? Ain't no woman crazy enough to try to ball and chain no man no more, y'all. Her stupid self-did it to herself. Case closed because she chose to allow it and put up with it for years. Why would any man buy the cow when he could use the milk up for free? It just ain't make no sense to Shabria at all. Ricoe was paying her greedy tail two-hundred dolla's a week to watch her two babies. Come on Sis, you only had to watch them three, maybe four days a week. Shabria lucked up and got her a good a*s man this time and her mama was still b*tching and complaining. *Her old tail*

need to sit down somewhere and do a crossword, **thought Shabria. Ain't make no sense how her Mama Tawanda was just getting over on a decent brutha like that.**

"Well, all righty then Trina. Girl, suit yourself. I just don't know why you came to act all stuck-up and anti-social. It's too f*cking hot for all that. We got non-alcoholic shit too, Trina! We is turning it out today in these here projects, Sis," said Shabria. By the look on Neicy's smug face, Shabria could tell that she knew what time it was. It was time to get they party started for real. Shabria couldn't help but feel a lil bit bad for her girls.

Here, she had this bomb a*s man doing the world for her and both of them was crazy in love with each other and sh*t. That love sh*t was so ridiculous and out of the blue for the both of them. Here, Shabria had that one king that was doing right by her and her two kids. Ricoe was taking her kids places they ain't never been or seen before. Her wallet ain't never allowdit for no Chuckie who! Wasn't no Chuckie Cheese or nothing like that in her tight a*s budget. Her man was handling his business like a boss all the time. Even down to this here ghetto a*s BBQ, thought Shabria. He ain't even have to do all that because he ain't even f*ck with none of those tenants in her building like that. Ricoe insisted on doing the damn thang, so she had no choice but to let her man be great. It's always going to be hate and pissy attitudes no matter what, thought Shabria. So, f*ck it. All she wanted to do was love on her man in private. It ain't feel right boasting all on her boo thang all in they faces. But they'll live and just have to deal with it. ***Sh*t, I know they want a man like mines for they self,*** **thought Shabria.**

The cookout was really jumping too. Everybody in the hood was enjoying themselves. Wasn't nobody else worrying about

no police but Trina's simple tail. Y'all should have seent her a*s all paranoid and sh*t and it was the weekend, too. Trina was all peeping around over people's shoulder's and sh*t and fidgeting like a fiend. Shabria just wanted her friend to chill and roll up a blunt or something. They had might as well enjoyed themselves because they might not get the opportunity again. Ordinarily, one might expect Trina's a*s to snitch. Shabria and Neicy knew for a fact that they girl wasn't like that on gawd, for real. Just simple as sh*t, that's all. No more and no less. Her and Trina both could tell that Neicy was a little bit tipsy and that agitated the hell out of Trina.

"I'm about ready to roll out. When black people get a lil' liquor in them, they start showing they a*sses in public and sh*t," complained Trina. "Y'all know these fools in these projects don't know how to act and it's hot a*s sh*t out here, too. I just ain't trying to be here when the police come and raid y'alls sh*t, Shabria. Cause you know they a*sses is going to start fighting and shooting and sh*t, Sis. We is damn near thirty. We is too old to still be cutting up like this," said Trina. Neicy put her middle finger up at Trina and rolled her eyes at her.

"Then take your old, negative Nancy hating a*s on outta here then, trick. We is supposed to be here for our m*therf*cking girl right here regardless. I want to know where your loyalty lies. You know Shabria a*s been dying to spill the tea on her new man to us and sh*t for a hot second now. We ain't had no fire a*s girl talk in a minute now, hoe," screamed Neicy's stupid tail. Neicy was the only Bonafede and proud hoe in the entire f*cking projects. Shabria and Trina still let her carry on though. Shabria really did want to brag on her man just a little bit. Sh*t, she was drunk in love now herself.

Shabria was blushing as she spoke to her right hand girls. Her and Ricoe was secretly blowing kisses to each other when they thought nobody else was looking and sh*t. Even pretty boy Ricoe was cheesing at his girl. He looked at Shabria like she was the only girl in the world for him. That sh*t right there gave her shivers and sh*t. All goosebumps kinds of sh*t. It was one of those feelings that every chick out here should experience at least once in her life, y'all. Ain't nothing like meeting the "one."

"See, y'all know your girl was about ready to give up on finding love, right! It's like something that I can't even began to explain in words. I'm like how and why is he here? Ricoe finishes my sentences and sh*t for me. He be knowing what I'm thinking, like how! This love of ours is so new. I got to pinch myself to see if my a*s is dreaming or not. I just love me some him like that. He do everything for me. He stay dropping bands on us and everything like a man should."

"Ricoe is paying my rent and my car insurance. The other day he said he going to give me money to open my own salon! Y'all know what that means right? Y'all my m*therf*cking girls, so you know I got you, Loves," cheesed Shabria as she felt them damn butterflies in her stomach again. Trina was down for the salon but still that Trina had to f*ck it up as usual.

Trina stayed quiet and listened. She wanted to be there for her bestie no doubt. Trina didn't believe in that love at first sight crap though. *Ain't no way in hell them two are that head over heels in love,* thought Trina to herself. *Maybe lust or infatuation.* "Girl, it sounds good and shit. But what do his a*s do though? If his job is hiring, put a sista on for real! Ain't nobody in the hood slinging dough like Ricoe. And he ain't no drug dealer either, Bria," said Trina. Neicy got up because she wasn't feeling sis funky lil'

attitude about her girl's new man. Her tipsy, clumsy a*s almost fell on the poor girl.

"What the f*ck Trina? Why is you all nosey and sh*t for? Why is you worrying about what her man is or is not doing? Dang, can yo' a*s at least pretend to be happy for once in yo' miserable a*s life, Trina? Our sista was the first one to fall in love out the group and sh*t. Let Bria have her moment. Yours will come, damn. Bria, you ain't got to answer this b*tch if you don't want to. It ain't none of our business for real!" yelled Neicy spilling her drink all over herself. It was about to be an a*s whipping up in there between them now.

"Naw, Trina is right. Y'all my sistas from another muva. I ain't going to lie and sh*t. When I met my man, he said he do. Wayment, I don't even know. Y'all my yellow, crazy a*s been f*cking with this man for two months and don't know shit about what he do, lol! It don't matter though cause he ain't in the streets. We together day and night, a'ight," said Shabria sounding real stupid.

"My point exactly. I'm just saying, Bria. You just met yo and he already been around your kids. If MamaTawanda don't like his a*s, it has to be a reason. Just be careful a'ight. Baltimore City has been off the chains this year. If his a*s is really worth gold, then a'ight that's on you! I guess yo' a*s learnt enough about him then. I can't say sh*t cause I don't know of dude like that," said Trina all serious like. Neicy wouldn't just shut the f*ck up and let it go.

"Bria, forget her jealous, hating a*s. This is your time to shine. Today is all about you and your man. Adjust yo' crown my Queen. Haters gonna hate. These thots want what they can't have. Who wouldn't want to take your place, Girl? That jealousy

sh*t is always the root of all evil. Realistically, these ratchet a*s hoes ain't never going to be happy for you! Look at you all glowing and shit, Girl! If I was you, I would shout it out to the world too. You hit the lotto on that one and you got to take him all the way to the bank too, a'ight!" said Neicy. Shabria was feeling everything but that last part though. *I ain't no f*cking gold-digger though,* thought Bria to herself.

"Oh, I ain't worrying about what these hoes think, Neicy. I just don't want to be showing off too much though. You feel me. Do y'all think this cookout was a bit too much, huh? I don't want the tenants feeling bad and sh*t about their own current situations. My mans was only trying to help out for real. Know what I mean, ladies. Sh*t, somebody had to look out for them right Cherry Land Realty don't give a f*ck about us for real," and Shabria continued.

"Section eight is paying damn near double the rent to these b*tches and for what? None of us ain't got sh*t to show for it! Ricoe is over there throwing down on the m*therf*cking grill all by his damn self. He ain't even ask for sh*t in return from nobody out here. That's how good my man is. Ain't nobody even have to contribute a dime this shit."

"Ain't none of these cheap a*s hoes had to pick-up no paper plates or cups from the dollar store or nothing this time. I ain't being petty but damn! Everybody and they mama and daddy out here. Ricoe got hookah and even fireworks for they children. That sh*t is still illegal but my mans still copped it for these thots and sh*t. These b*tches got a real nerve to be salty and jealous for real," yelled Shabria. Neicy a*s still was right. Her man's good deeds ain't mean sh*t to them tenants. They just there to get they eat on. F*ck Ricoe and his generosity. Shabria noticed

that both her girls had a crazy look on their faces. Neicy bold a*s spoke out first. She felt like pretty a*s Shabria still ain't get the point. The alcohol had gotten the best of her now. She got that her bestie Bria was all in love and sh*t. But the grease had hit the pan and it was about to be a serious burst of flames. Neicy took a bite off her Italian Sausage and was ready to flip the script. *Oh lordt, her drunk a*s is f*cked up again.*

"Hold the fuck up. Y'all shut-up and listen to what whore a*s Neicy gots to say for a change. I can speak my mind too! I want to know why you b*tches don't love my a*s for real. I am sick of you b*tches thinking I is stupid and sh*t. I'm a proud ass throat baby and what. I love what I do in them streets. My name Neicy and I like to f*ck and what. Ain't nobody ever love my a*s like that. I learnt this f*ck sh*t from my daddy. Yup, Dennis Lesley was a male whore that ain't work a day in his life. His a*s still don't. He f*cks for a career just like his baby girl right here. His a*s stayed entertaining attached or married b*tches. He liked being the center of attention just like me," and Neicy started hollering and crying. Her a*s loved causing a scene a scene and sh*t. Black people always had that one fool in the group that lived for cutting up and her name is Denise f*cking "Neicy" Lesley. Proud whore when her a*s is sober and drunk as a b*tch. When that a*s was drunk though, it was never no accountability on her part. Shabria and Trina ran to comfort their girl.

"Neicy, we love your a*s just the way you is. Ain't no shaming and judgement zones over here. Girl, you got to do what makes you happy! As long as yo' ass ain't fucking with my n*gga that is! Ain't that right, Trina?" said Shabria and she gave her a look to kill. Like your black a*s better co-sign with a sista or else type of stare. Slowly, her a*s caught on.

"Yeah Sis, how you live your life is up to you. I get it. Your own father was responsible for part of it and sh*t. If it makes you happy, we is happy for yo' ass. Who got the right to tell you how to live yo' life, Denise Lesley?" co-signed Trina finally. Neicy a*s ain't pay they a*ses no attention though. The only voice she heard was hers. They was in they own private part of the courtyard. Wasn't nobody worrying about them three hoes.

"Y'all, think I give a shit bout having three cents in my chain purse, huh? Them men give me all the attention in the world when I'm on my knees. Ain't nothing like a lil' d*ck on the side, a'ight! You feel me? What I do ain't for the average hoe! Ain't like I had a daddy at home to tell me right from wrong. How could he anyway, he was and still is a male hoe. At least I got a little something from switching up from man to man. The next one gave up a couple of dollas and the one after him did too. I don't give a damn what these other hoes in this streets is doing, a'ight! It ain't always about get your hair and nails did. How many b*tches can vouch for that? I only wish they would cuddle with my a*s after they nut. It ain't like a thot got roaches in they bed. But even that dream is getting played out. Sure, I want some bacon and eggs from McDonald's after I f*ck sometimes. I'm a'ight with that shit now because I don't have no choice. The problem is these hoes always pointing the blame on the side chick. I ain't bragging on being a homewrecker but her man is to blame too. If he ain't wearing his ring, why the f*ck should I care? Why the side chick gotta respect the main chick, y'all?"

"That man made a decision to leave his woman's bed to come lay in mines. I ain't never had to put no gun to no m*therf*cker's head, a'ight! A lil' community d*ck on the side ain't never hurt nobody. What I do ain't for every woman like I said. I get that, y'all."

Saying that out loud hit differently for Neicy. But it is what it is at the end of the day. Her girls had her back and that was all that mattered. Shabria and Trina made it their business to show they girl some love. After all the crying, runny noses and Neicy passing gas, they was a'ight again.

Shabria took the silence as a time to reflect on herself. She couldn't believe that she a'int know nair one of her neighbors like that. They kids a'int even play together like that and they all went to the same school. Shabria shook her head at all the strange people chopping down on grilled steaks and burgers. They was tearing them hotdogs apart like they was going out of style. Them dudes was sucking on them crab legs like they lives depending on it and shit. When Shabria looked over at the grill, her man was smiling at her. *Oh God, do I love me some him,* thought Shabria. It was something about the way that Ricoe looked at her that causes her flickering heart to beat faster. It was one of those things that neither of them could describe for real. Now, Trina had to get one more thing off her chest too. This time, about her girl, Shabria. Trina was hesitant at first but sh*t needed to be said.

"Bria, don't get me wrong, Sis. This sh*t right here is lit as f*ck. You and your man's intentions was right on time and sh*t. Just not sincere. I think even Neicy's drunk a*s can vouch for that. Y'alls timing was just way off. If it was really for the tenant's benefit, why not f*cking grill at the end of the month? You could have waited just two more weeks to celebrate y'alls two month anniversary."

"By the end of the months, they a*s will be scrapping crumbs out the corners of cupboards and sh*t. These people got pink

eviction notices and sh*t on they door. Dates and holidays matter in the ghetto. Flaunting you and yo' man's love like this is doing what for these tenants, huh? Half these people gots they electric cut off and sh*t," said Trina.

Neicy turned her head out of embarrassment because that sh*t really was true. The streets was going to be talking about her yellow a*s by the morning time. She might as well know that sh*t now and but a band aid on her bruised ego. ***Just suck that sh*t up with a straw and keep that shit moving,*** **Sis, thought Neicy.**

"Sis, it is true. Y'alls timing was just a little bit off. Next time do sh*t when people need it the most! You in a zone and shit. I get that, Bria. Just don't forget about your girls, a'ight" said drunk Neicy. Shabria grabbed the Henny bottle and took a long hard slurp. She was pissed with both of them for real.

"Y'all both can kiss my ass, a'ight! Do you know how ridiculous and stupid y'all sound? So, because I lucked up and snagged a man with money, I owe the hood. Get the fuck outta here. Me or my man a'int responsible for shit around here, a'ight. Nobody tell them hoes to have all those deadbeat baby daddies. How can you keep making babies that yo' ass can't take care of and be looking for handouts? So, I guess the Fourth of July party got to be on July 30th because they can't eat until the first of the month. Who has a guy laying up in they crib in 2021 that a'int paying shit? These thots and single baby mama's a'int shit!" screamed Shabria. She turned all red and evil looking. A couple of ladies heard her trifling ass and rolled out. Shabria had rubbed her girls the wrong way too. Chicks always assumed that the next chick had to be jealous and salty when it wasn't even like that for real.

"Bitch, how yo' ass going forget where you came from like that? You a single, baby mama too. Your red-bone ass get a man

with a couple of dollas and go crazy. How you gonna stand there and put your sisters down like that, Bria? You got a wet ass for two months. Just two months and you already done lost yo' mind, Girl. You don't know them lady's situation to trash talk them all out in the open like that. That's what's wrong with black people today! Especially us sista girls. We stay putting each other down instead of lifting each other up," shouted Neicy. Trina stood up and was about ready to roll out her damn self.

"Shabria Reid, you foul as shit for that one. You want the tenants to kiss your ass for some fucking hotdogs and macaroni salad now. You a'int discreet about yo' shit or nothing. You a'int have to be all loud and ignorant like that. I mean they was literally sitting right over there. That man a'int no good if he changing yo' ass out like that. I was about to fix a plate, too. I ain't even hungry no more, a'ight. I don't want no man that's going to have me showing my ass in disrespecting my sistas like that. I gotta get outta here, y'all," and Trina straight walked away. Shabria just stood there looking real crazy. People was starting to leave and shit. Shabria had the nerve to look at Neicy like you got me.

"Naw Sis, you fucked the BBQ up all by yo' damn self. No caption is needed. I a'int got shit to say to you for real," and Neicy turned around in her chair so her back was facing her. Shabria realized that she may had ran her mouth a little too much. It was just her in her feeling and she felt the need to put her two cents in. *Shit, if the shoe fit then wear it then. I'm sick of all them for real. They made the choice to live like that, not me. I don't owe them nothing for real,* thought Shabria.

Neicy and Trina had a nerve because all they do is talk shit about they ass too and got the nerve to call her out on it like she was the only one doing wrong. *All three of us done sat on my hood a many of nights and talked mad shit about them trifling ladies that lived in my apartment building now. Old nasty ass Neicy, maybe even quiet Trina is probably fucking they man on the low. Just ain't no telling with these hoes*, thought Shabria. Shabria wasn't about to kiss her ass because she was dead wrong for all that.

"Come on now, Neicy don't be like that. It a'int nothing but the alcohol in me talking. You know I a'int cruddy like that, Sis. A'int shit I can do about it now. I a'int mean to call nobody out like that," and Shabria started crying.

"Fuck a crocodile tear, Hoe. I a'int like that shit. Especially since yo' ass is cut from the same cloth. Yo' ass is stupid anyway. I a'int switching up for no man that technically a'int even official. Baby Girl, at least get your ring first. Any man out hear with no wedding band is definitely still for the streets. You all up on that high horse and shit. Yo' ass might wind up just like that fool over there. Look at his black ass on that grill. All anti-social and shit. That's gonna be yo' ass. Watch and see, Sis," said Neicy.

"See, it a'int even like that for real. Yo' ass always got to be blowing shit outta proportion. Y'all hoes expect his ass to do this and that, right. My new man supposed to grill and entertain yo' asses too, now. Just because he' a'int ghetto and all up in y'all faces, he's anti-social right, dummy! Neicy, I be glad when you get a man of your own because yo' ass a'int nothing but trouble, lol and yo' ass still a'int shit." Neicy laughed with her girl but on a whole other level though.

Shabria didn't even catch it. Neicy stood up and bent over so all eyes was on her, including her man. She wiggled her ass to get Ricoe's attention. While he was blowing kisses at Shabria, he was licking his lips at her. Even now and Shabria's dumb tail a'int catch it again. *What am I going to do about my besties' new man? He is clearly thirsty and drooling over my every move as it is. If this is what being in love is I don't want it. Throw all that phoney ass shit away. Her man is for the streets. I tried to tell her and shit. I even said it loud enough for the hoes in the back,* thought Neicy to herself.

"Oh, I surely don't need my own bae because I got everybody else's man as it is, Love. One day y'all hoes gonna find out the hard way. Ain't nobody loyal no more. I definitely would know because I have always been about that life. A'int shit change about it. Just another day and a new taken nigga to fuck with. Besides, I a'int the tied down type of chick. I do's me and whatever else I got a taste for, a'ight," said Neicy all nasty. Shabria looked over to see if her man was looking at Neicy's phat ass. Everybody else was but not her boo though. Shabria knew for a fact that her man wouldn't go near trash like her. Ricoe was a fine man of substance and class. *A black, middle-class professional with a good head on his shoulders,* thought Shabria to herself.

Neicy got up all phony to give her girl a hug like they still cool after all that. Shabria was the needy type so she was all with it. Neicy was just ready to get the party started again.

"Sis, we is good. Alcohol make yo' ass say and do stupid shit. A'int nobody knows that more than me. The baby mamas will get over this shit. Just let it die down a lil bit. It'll be alright, Girl. Trina's ass too. It's a rumor going around that her parents are getting divorced after thirty years of marriage.

"Her stupid grown ass moping around like a little ass girl. Shit happens and everything is made of glass. Trina need to get over that shit. Her ass is too old to be acting simple about some damn divorce. That bitch is pushing up on the dirty thirty as it is. Me and you had to grow up in a single fucking parent home and our ass is a'ight. I a'int fin to cradle no big ass woman. Unless she trying to suck these titties now," said Neicy's nasty self. Shabria was starting to question her girl's sexual identity. *Is her ass in the closet or what? I a'int gotta problem if her ass is bi. Her ass could have told me that shit from the get because she will always be my girl regardless. Inquiring minds want to know. Her ass stay beating around the Mulberry Bush for no fucking reason. It's stupid if you asked me,* thought Shabria.

"Bitch, you is just nasty for no reason. You know that. I can't with you sometimes. All you know is sucking and fucking, Girl. At some point though, yo' ass gonna have to throw in the towel. Your ass is getting to old too to be out here thotting and shit. Girl, you is almost pushing thirty. Don't you want to settle down and have a family of your own one day?" asked Shabria.

"Why is I got to do all that for? You and Trina is my fucking family. We share everythang, a'ight! Only besties can share a love like that. Come on now, we done shared toothbrushes and panties before, Bria now. If that a'int nasty, I don't know what is," said Neicy seductively. Shabria felt a rush of embarrassment all of a sudden. It was so bad that her cheeks turned blood red but she still was smiling a lil' bit. That shit right there was actually turning Neicy's fast ass on. Shabria could tell. It was all in the eyes.

"Girl, stop it! You is too much. We a'int never do no nasty shit like that ever," pleaded Shabria.

Her nasty ass is getting the fuck out of hand now. She is doing too much now. Like what is all this for? I ain't trying to get down with her ass like that. I got a whole man and her ass knows that already, thought Shabria. "I a'int about to wear another bitches drawls now. Enough with that already. For real though, I feel bad for our girl. It don't matter how old she is, Neicy. That shit still hurts. That's all she knows. I feel for her. You and I is gonna still be there for her, you dig?" and Shabria was dead serious. Neicy wasn't paying her any attention. She was too busy texting somebody else's man as usual. Shabria focused her attention back on that sexy, sweaty chocolate brother firing up the grill. His ass looked like a snack all shirtless and shit. Shabria licked her lips like she wanted to eat him up alive. Her and her man was so busy eyeballing each other and blowing kisses that she was out of tune. Neither of the ladies realized that a homeless man had rolled up on them. He got all up in they personal space like it was nobody's business for real. Neicy caught it and was ready to bring the heat for real. She damn near had to shake Bria's silly ass back to reality.

"Yo, Bria. You a'int tell me yo' daddy was invited. What it do old man? Is you her daddy or something rolling all up on us and shit. I mean yo' stanking ass is all up in our personal space," said Neicy. Shabria turned to see if her man had caught that shit for real. She looked up and his black ass had gone ghost. Shabria was like what. Her man just up and disappeared out the blue. *His ass been firing up the grill all day. Why would he just up and leave the grill unattended like that,* thought Shabria? Her man did a pop-up Houdini on her ass. Shabria was like, what the fuck?

"I heard you crack slick dummy! Don't be denying yo' sugar daddy in public like that. Show some respect for Papi now! Yo' ass is already spending his SSI," laughed Shabria.

"Yo' ass know he's one of yo' married men checking up on that ass. But for real though Sir, what's good? The shelter is two blocks down the street. Once you get to that light right there,

make a left. Christopher's place is right there, a'ight. Since yo' ass is here, let me fix you a plate. Catch my man over there before he start throwing away the leftovers. Just eat it while you walking because you can't bring food in there. At least, that's what Neicy said when she was hoeing up there," and Shabria started dying laughing.

"Hold the fuck up Sis! Yo' ass is foul as shit. Now why, would I be giving a homeless man some coochie now? Look at his ran over shoes. He looked like he ain't shaved or bathed since before Christ. Look at that sad receding hairline with those buck ass teeth, Sis. Looking like a short, stubby beaver and shit. Come on now, Sis! This is Neicy yo' ass is talking to trash to. Whoever fucking this piece of shit needs to be thrown in the trash? Throw both they asses back to the gutter," said Neicy.

The homeless man kept his eyes on Ricoe the whole time. Shabria thought maybe it could have been one of his peeps or something. It's a small world because everybody know everybody for real.

"Sis, you is cray cray! Fool, you heard my girl. Now get to stepping. We a'int even supposed to be out here carrying on this long. Yo' ass about to get all us in trouble for real. Just take yo' shit and bounce or else, old man! Wayment, why yo' ass a'int moving, Sir?" said Neicy seriously.

The homeless man was bold as shit because he didn't budge at all. He was bold as fuck too. He saw Neicy's gun and still wasn't scared.

"You mean, one of you ladies is fucking with that clown ass, Remy Jackson. Oh shit! I thank you ladies kindly for the food but I didn't come over here to disrespect y'all. I got business with that black ass man that was on the grill. Remy's ass owe me

money and I a'int leaving until I get it. Old blackie owes me for services not rendered. I'm here on official street business, Miss. This ain't got shit to do with y'all, a'ight. His ass got a nerve to be out here showing face like that. I can't forget a face like that on gawd! I know his black ass saw me standing here. I don't know what his fucking problem is. Y'all tell Remy trifling ass that Tyrone need to holla at him about something. I a'int mean to disturb you pretty ladies. I hope neither of y'all is caught up in his shit. He a'int no good, trust me cause I know his ass like that. Old Remy Jackson back showing his ass in Baltimore City again. Fucking unbelievable. He gonna get fucked up over here in East Baltimore Projects," said the homeless dude. Neicy put her hand to her mouth and was loving all the drama.

"Oh, Sis this is some juicy shit right here. Yo' man even got a homeless man checking for him now. I done seen and heard it all now. Like that song goes, Shabria. Oops, he better call "Tyrone." Call him. That used to be the shit back in the day. Sis, how you gonna handle this with yo' man m.i.a, huh?" said Neicy while cracking up. But for Shabria this was no laughing matter at all. That's why she a'int fuck with nobody in her hood. Somebody was always hating and starting shit for no reason. Shabria wanted to know why they had it out for her new man though. Ricoe a'int even know nobody around there.

Or at least that's what he claimed. Him running out like that a'int look too good. Shabria tried to smooth things over politely with the hobo. *This homeless man is serious as shit over somebody named Remy Jackson and shit. He ain't trying to leave or nothing,* thought Shabria.

"Hoe, remind me why we is friends again! I'm about two seconds away from beating that ass. You feel me. How about I just

call my man ova here to straighten this shit out, a'ight damn! Look you need to fucking fall back. Ain't no man in this joint named a Remy. If yo' ass keeps going on about this foolishness, you gonna make my man catch a charge, a'ight!" yelled Shabria.

"Chill, Shabria! It's obvious that he came all the way over here for a reason. Let's at least hear the man out, a'ight. He ain't asking for shit else, right. He just saying he know Ricoe that's all!" Neicy couldn't hold her laughter in any longer.

"Bitch, do yo' dumb ass have to put my man's government name all out in the street like that? What the fuck is wrong with you, Neicy? We don't even know this homeless dude like that and my man damn sure wouldn't fuck with a homeless bum like this, Neicy. This isn't funny and yo' ass is starting to piss me off!" shouted Shabria. Ricoe not showing face was really starting to tick her off now. ***So, I guess his ass wanna act like he's deaf and blind over on that grill. Fuck flipping burgers and shit cause yo' ass need to be over here handling yo' business, and boss the fuck up for real,*** **thought Shabria.**

"Oh, so that's what he calls himself now. A fucking Ricoe! Miss, I know faces and like I said Remy, Ricoe whoever he calls himself fucking owes me and that's that, a'ight," he said.

"Sir, I apologize for this misunderstanding. But there is no Remy person here," said Shabria feeling stupid as hell.

My man needs to be over here taking care of this piece of shit for real. As a man that is only expected of him. How his ass gonna fall short and fall back all the sudden, **thought Shabria? "You know they say we all look alike and that's all it is for real. I was nice enough to offer you a hot plate. Shit, take two. We have more than enough to go around. We a'int stingy over here! So, why don't you go on. The person you think you saw is not here,**

a'ight," said Shabria. She was actually a little bit scared and beyond confused. Shabria wanted to know more about that dude for some reason.

"Miss, I a'int here for no food. I been eating out of trashcans and dumpsters since I met up with Remy's black ass. That's what Remy does best. And ain't nothing wrong with that. He just fucked me over big time. I slipped up by trusting his black ass so that's on me. You have no idea of what you getting yourself into. Do you? As a man, I'm telling you to cut him loose. Like I said, high yella , that fool owes me. I'm about to get real ignent up in here! You see, Remy is hiding from me, right red bone! Ask yourself mommy, why is that?" shouted the homeless man.

Neicy was looking at her all crazy. I told you so was written all over her smug face. Shabria played it off. She wasn't about to take no L in front of her like that.

"I forgot my man said he had an important conference call this evening. Let me holla at him first in private. He'll come over here and you can meet him and finally see for' yourself. I ain't gotta lie about no dumb shit and neither does my man for real. I a'int want to do this shit in front of all these people like that. But I will though so you can shut the fuck up, old man. You feel me?" lied Shabria. Neicy started blushing and smiling and shit. Ricoe's sexy ass was approaching them out the blue.

Ricoe came over smiling with two plates in his hand. Both ladies couldn't deny that her man fixed them a mean plate. He packed on some BBQ ribs, auntie's potato salad, devil eggs and extra heavy cheesy mac and cheese.

Shabria was feeling some type of way about all of that. This was the first time she was introducing her man to her bestie and some fool named Tyrone at the same time. *Like what is the odds,*

thought Shabria? For a long time, Shabria was hesitant about that shit and then on a day like this of all days. It's not every day that a man like Ricoe Jones slides in. Besides, it wasn't her man that she didn't trust. It was her homegirl for real and Neicy to be exact. Ain't no girl out here want another man cheesing all up in the next girl's face. Then, homeless ass fucking Tyrone is in the joint too.

Shabria thought she was hallucinating. She thought she saw Neicy all smiling up in her man face. *Shabria get it together because you know yo' girl ain't like that a'ight. Just because she a thot, Neicy already know that yo' man is off limits.* Shabria had all these crazy thoughts in her head. She was in a daze and not really watching anything or anybody in particular. But when she snapped out of it, her jealousy bar went up real high because her boo was smiling all at Neicy. *This is the type of shit that made you rip out yo' girl's weave and beat that ass,* thought Shabria. *His ass even had the nerve to act like he ain't see the homeless dude at all. Really, what the fuck, Ricoe? His ass is for the birds,* thought Shabria.

"Lovely ladies, I noticed y'all ain't try Ricoe's signature plates yet." Ricoe glanced over at Tyrone ass and kept on rapping and shit. "Bae, it looks like yo' sister girl want to taste it real bad. I've been told that all it takes is one lick. I got that fire to get you addicted and like what."

"I be known to get yo' panties twisted and shit. My thing is delicious. Imagine how my sauce drips off my meat," said Ricoe who was clearly saying and doing too much. Shabria thought it was a fucked up first introduction. *Ricoe's black ass a'int have no shame, dignity or nothing,* thought Shabria and he continued his shenanigans, too. "I make you wanna suck it off my bone

and shit. I will having yo' ass lose yo' mind," and he seductively licked his lips. Shabria looked at Neicy and her hot ass was melting. Mad, Shabria snatched both places from him and tossed it on the nearby folding table. Neicy and Ricoe started laughing like they shared an inside joke together and Bria felt left out.

"Hold the fuck up! You serving yo' dick on a platter or food, Bae? I can't tell by the way my homegirl's mouth is watering. All that shit ain't even necessary for real. Sex on a platter now, Ricoe! And yo' ass got company. Bae, this man right here say he know yo' ass and shit. I done told him yo' ain't who he thinks yo' ass is already" yelled Shabria out of jealously. Neicy could see why she was pissed off, too. Neicy being her right hand had decided to tap in on that delicious looking dick platter. But Tyrone stinking ass crushed that fantasy for real. Tyrone ignent ass was ready to tear shit up, a'ight.

"Old black ass Remy Jackson in the flesh, huh. A meeting with the devil himself. Who would have thought that I would have lived to see this .? I thought yo' grimy ass was burning in hell," said homeless Tyrone. Even Neicy ignored his ignent ass. She wanted to talk about sexting and shit instead.

"You know that's fucked up, right! All that sexual innuendo and references ain't even necessary, Sir. Yo' ass is suggesting head right in my girl's face like that, too" said Neicy.

"Especially, in front of a single hoe like me. I ain't even been properly introduced and yo' ass is already showing out and is extra nasty!" said Neicy while trying to hide her excitement. She was sick and in need of some TLC from her best friend's man. Oh, *I'm definitely going down on this type of head doctor. I'm about ready to swallow all his pills all over my face for real.* "Shabria, yo' ass betta get this man," said Neicy yelling and smiling at the same time. Shabria didn't know who ass to jump in first for it. Her bestie or her new man. Ricoe ain't give her a chance to overreact though. Tyrone was pissed how they all just ignored his ass like he wasn't outside with them and shit. *These young people better recognize! I is homeless not fucking invisible,* thought Tyrone. Ricoe ain't even look his way for real. Shabria was wondering what in the hell twilight zone was going on at that here ratchet ass cookout.

"What had happened was y'alls mind is in the gutter. Both of you is nasty as fuck if you asked me. Neicy yo' ass need to get yo' eyes off my print in my gray sweats. Only my girl should be thirsting like that. Sweetheart, what the fuck is wrong with Neicy's ass, right? I see why yo' ass ain't want us to meet. For the record, I'm a damn chef and a poet," said Ricoe. *This right here. Come on now. Oh, this fool is a comedian, pathological liar and a whack ass Houdini all in one,* thought Tyrone.

Neicy ain't want too, but decided to take it there anyway. There wasn't no way her girl ain't see through his lies and fuckery. *Ain't that much love in the world,* thought Neicy. She was about to speak but he cut her straight off and continued.

"Excuse me, but I am still speaking hoe! I intelligently and creatively know how to satisfy both worlds. I got all types of talents. I was just being poetic, damn!" yelled Ricoe.

"Y'all project people don't know nothing about literature and poetry at all. That's fucking sad as shit for real! Neicy, I see yo' ass about some stupid shit, huh? Fuck the plate! Go on and let that shit simmer then with yo' illiterate ass," yelled Ricoe. Neicy drunk ass got all in his face and refused to back down. Shabria tried to pull her back but Neicy was ready to wild out on her man. *That man right there is still crazy as shit. Ain't nothing change but a chicken wing,* thought Tyrone. *Maybe, I should leave that lunatic the fuck alone for real* was in his thoughts again. Neicy ain't want her girl laying hands on her like that. Neicy was about to ready to beat both they asses. All Tyrone could do was shake his head at that point. *These young people today ain't worth shit,* thought Tyrone. They continued to cut up.

"Naw, get the fuck off me, Sis! His black ass called me a hoe. He don't even know me like that, Bria! He standing here lying on me and shit right in yo' face, Girl. What yo' ass going to do about it, huh? I'm about ready to take my own weave out and fuck dude ass up? I know yo' ass got me, right," yelled Neicy. Ricoe got right back in her face and was ready to pop her in the mouth. Shabria quickly got in the middle of them.

"What we ain't gonna do is get nobody locked up tonight. It's too hot for all this shit for real. We can't never have a lil' get together without somebody ass acting a fool. Ain't nobody need to go to no central booking tonight, a'ight! Don't make no fucking sense, y'all! And Bae, I see that yo' ass don't know how to act right in front of company. How rude? You know that? Like who, the fuck is this here homeless dude for real? He clearly ain't invisible because he reeks of sitting creek water and mud," shouted Shabria.

"Like, why does he think he know you, Bae? I ain't gonna keep asking yo' black ass, a'ight," yelled Shabria and threw her hands up. Ricoe snatched Shabria up real close and whispered in her ear. He was tied of her always bitching and complaining.

"Wayment, Bae! Explain to me why yo' ass is entertaining this piece of shit again? I don't find this shit fucking funny or cute. I'm over there busting my ass to please you and yo' ass gonna do some fucked up shit like this. I'm starting to think that

yo' ass don't appreciate shit I do around here for real. Yo' ungrateful ass is starting to get under my skin, a'ight. I took a day off work for this crap!" whispered Ricoe like he was the victim. Shabria wiggled free of his grip and got right back on his ass.

"I is appreciating it all. That ain't got nothing to do with that homeless man though. I got my kids around here playing and shit. Do something! If it's a mistaken identity, tell his ass then, Ricoe. Don't hate the messenger, a'ight. His ass said yo' name is Remy, not me. Don't get shitty with me! You is doing yo' thang with the ghetto BBQ, I get that. Yo' ass spassed out in hooked the tenants up with all this food and shit. I did offer to contribute so it is what it is. My ass don't get no fucking orange EBT card and I got two kids, a'ight. I was doing the damn thang before yo' ass, a'ight. How is ignoring the man going to solve it though? I ain't gonna spend the rest of my evening dancing around on eggshells either. This right here ain't got shit to do wit me or nobody else out here, Ricoe. Protect me and my kids, Bae and handle yo' shit," said Shabria. Ricoe stood there with a dumb look on his face all quiet and shit. Neicy couldn't believe the circus show happening before her eyes.

"So, who's the fool, now? Yo' man is clearly out of line and disrespecting you, Shabria. How yo' ass not going to do shit about it, Shabria?" Angry and frustrated, Neicy turned to face Ricoe because Shabria was standing there looking stupid as hell. "Ricoe, it ain't like she gotta be thirsty fool! Street trash like yo' ass come a dime a dozen. Yo' ass ain't even all that for real. Shabria is pretty as shit as it is. She ain't got to take no shit from any man for real. None of us do! Yo' black ass need to take yo' anger out on the source of the problem, Tyrone periodt! Shit at this point, Sis throw the whole man in the trash. You seen him come

on to me, right. Right, Shabria. I know yo' ass ain't blind or deaf now. A lil' bit slow but fuck all that. You is vouching for me right over him. Wayment, yo' ass ain't saying shit! Why is that Bria?" yelled Neicy. Shabria couldn't decide who side she was on. By the grace of God, Ricoe finally decided to address the matter at hand to they surprise.

"I tell you what, Bae! I will holla at this kat for you, a'ight. I ain't got time for her shit today, Tyrone or whoever the fuck you is for real." Ricoe finally turned to Tyrone. Neicy noticed the odd way he looked at the homeless guy. *Tyrone was talking shit before so how come his ass is quiet now? What the fuck*, thought Neicy. *Something ain't right with this shit right here.* Ricoe kept right on running his mouth and wasn't talking about nothing. *His ass just liked to hear himself speak for real,* thought Neicy and Shabria. "This right here is a fucking private family affair. Yo' ass can't just walk up on a project function like that, Cuzzo. I don't even fuck with yo' ass like that. Yo' ass come on my premises and mad disrespect my girl and our kids. I'm going to need for yo' ass to meet me in the parking lot over there or else, a'ight."

Ricoe pointed to the parking lot pissed the fuck off. Tyrone a'int have no choice but to get his ass up outta there now. Tyrone did as he was told. He knew how that fool got down for real. That man was cold as ice. Ricoe turned on his lady next.

"As my girl, yo' ass supposed to check that bitch and put her in her fucking place. What the fuck, Bria? Stop being a weak ass bitch and boss the fuck up, Shabria. I ain't got time for these childish games, a'ight," said Ricoe. Neicy wasn't having that so she shot right back at him.

"Sha, is yo' ass really gonna let him talk down to me like that and do nothing about it? It's like that! When his black ass leave yo' ass, who got yo' back then? His ass gonna leave you just like the rest of them and then what. I said the shit and what? I am tied of being cordial with his black ass for yo' sake! All yo' mans do is attack me," said Neicy and she turned to look at him.

"Who hurt you, Boo? Because it damn sure wasn't me so why is you dissing me for? I don't even know yo' ass like that for real. What have I ever done to yo' ass to deserve this shit? A hurt nigga is a sorry ass nigga in my book. How yo' ass gonna stand there and expect my homegirl to side with yo' grimy ass, huh? Cause I already *know* what time it is! Shabria ain't ready for that convo! Her ass just ain't cut out for the streets like I is. On the strength though, fuck you Remy, Ricoe or whatever yo' name is!" and she attempted to spit on him but she missed. Ricoe turned his head just in time but that ain't stop him from knocking her head off. In an instant, he had Neicy on the grass and was sitting on her. Ricoe had his hands around her throat but wasn't really choking her though. Shabria and Tyrone rushed over to deescalate the problem. But to no avail because he clearly had the intent to kill her.

No doubt that he would have choked the shit out of her in a heartbeat. The homeless man was barely strong enough to pull him off her. Shabria was pulling her man back and thinking to herself. *I don't mean no harm but the bitch done asked for it. Calling a black man a nigga and spitting nasty on him too. If her trifling ass can't hold her liquor, her ass need to drink a soda then. A'int no man going to stand for that disrespectful bullshit. If my man is for the streets, that's my fucking business. I a'int ask for her opinion and shit as it is. Fuck looking out for me because yo' ass is already done start to piss me the fuck off too,* thought Shabria.

"Yung blood, yung blood listen to me now! Let it go, Remy!

This ain't what you want to do main man, trust me. What she did was fucked up shit, but the broad ain't worth it Yo'. Come holla at me before the man in blue get here, a'ight, "said Tyrone and he was finally able to lift him up. Ricoe got up and appeared to be out of it, like in a daze and shit. Neicy got up and grasped her neck with her hand in shock. The pain was throbbing and aching now. She couldn't believe how he fucked her up. That man was rough and savage as fuck and it turned her on. *Ain't nothing like a rough mutherfucker to whip that* ass *from time to time. His ass is gangsta and I definitely want him now. This hoe is sharing whether her ass like it or not! If we is girls like she claim, then why can't my ass be on the up and up too. He looks like his ass is slinging enough for both our asses as it is. Like they say a closed mouth don't get fed and shit.* thought, Neicy to herself. Torn between the both of them, Shabria did what any woman would do in that situation. She went to her man's side to be his peace. Ain't that expected of the main chick these days.

"Bae, is you ok?" said Shabria while trembling. "Can I get you a drink or something to eat? Let me holla at my girl while yo' ass deal with Tyrone, a'ight. You know I got you of course. Bae, can't we just drop this? Neicy is real sorry and I am, too. She ain't have to go all in on you like that. Neicy owes you a sincere apology. Disrespect ain't tolerated around here. Go on and fix you a plate or something, Bae," said Shabria. Her ass was real fucking confused and ain't know what to do for real. Fix her man the plate or not at this point because she didn't want to leave them alone because her and Tyrone could barely pull him off as it was. *Ain't no telling when his ass will go off again. This bad temper streak is out of control for real. What if he had killed her best friend? I ain't sign up to be in* love *with a killer now and be his accessory and shit.*

Neicy rolled her eyes and went the fuck off.

"Sorry my ass, Shabria Reid. Yo' man viciously attacked me and that hobo over there is a witness. What the fuck am *I* apologizing for? If I'm a hoe then his mama a trick crack hoe then! Ain't no man supposed to have us splitting and shit. What yo' ass need to do is get him to apologize to me first. His ass done fucked with the wrong one today! Fuck that. I ain't bowing down unless the paper is right!" yelled Neicy. Shabria wasn't nothing to play with either. She got right back on her nasty ass like it wasn't nothing for real.

"Neicy, our ass ain't lil' ass girls on no fucking playground no more. We is both getting to old for this shit now. Grow the fuck up, damn. We ain't playing hopscotch and dealing with no lil' ass boys, Neicy. We is grown now and fucking with real men now. All that childish dumb shit is played out. I done had my own kids and shit. I am a whole baby muva times two."

"What I look like still playing dumb ass games with you. I am so over you for real. If his ass was a dog, you'd be praising him and shit. That's yo' problem Neicy! Yo' ass need a man or something. Go to fucking trade school and do something with yo' life. Y'all miserable lonely bitches ain't shit!" Shabria had to catch herself before her mouth got her in trouble again.

A blind man could see that Shabria was scared to death. Shabria tried to pretend that she ain't have no parts in their argument for clout. She wanted Neicy to look like the bad guy but it backfired big time. Ricoe stood there pouting with his arms folded across his chest like a spoiled brat. He ain't been right since he heard his girl say fix yo' own plate and shit. Ricoe was like a bubbling volcano spilling lava at that point for real. Shabria ain't catch that mess but Neicy did. It was something how she was learning her bestie's man's ways like she was his soon to be girl already. *Ricoe, we is definitely connecting alright. After all this, his ass still expected her to fix his plate and serve him. Ain't that some shit,* thought Neicy.

"I'll make it real easy for yo' ass, Sis. What the fuck yo' ass mean by I should go fix a fucking plate? We is going to air our dirty laundry right the fuck here. I don't appreciate this shit, Bria. I'm a grown ass man when I'm paying yo' bills though right. So, don't handle me like I one of yo' kids, a'ight. I ain't complain when yo' ass memorized the pin to my credit cards though. Or when yo' ass write them checks in my name! All I be hearing is that yo' kids need this and need that mess, all the time. Yo' hands is always out for something or another. I ain't even complaining, am I? I manned up and took the role as they stepdaddy, right? So, ain't no competition with me and this hoe, is it?" yelled Ricoe. *Damn, my man is speaking the truth.*

I can't even lie. He was, and still is a good provider to my babies. Ain't no man ever take care of my household like Ricoe do. He stay buying us bulks of household items. He stay stocking me and my kids up with toilet tissue, paper towels, laundry and dish detergent, thought Shabria. *Neicy definitely can't compete with that. I'm tied of getting all my stuff that we need from the Dollar Store all the time. We is getting used to that quality name-brand shit now. I don't even have to worry about they toiletries either. I get my smell goods from Eastpoint Mall and shit now. Our skin is used to that Bath and Body Works. I ain't going back to no cheap ass cocoa butter,* thought Shabria. She was starting to feel real bad for blowing everything out of proportion like that in front of everybody like a fool. The whole BBQ got quiet when her man spoke. All eyes were glued on her new mysterious man. Even the fellas was peeping out how he moved. The bitter baby mamas just shook their head. Shabria had never felt so embarrassed like that in her whole life. Small crowds were forming now. A few of those greedy crumb snatchers had a nerve to be filming them live on Facebook. Shabria tried to grab Ricoe's arm and whisper in his ear, but he wasn't trying to hear that shit. Ricoe just pushed her hands away in disgust.

"I don't get it, Shabria! Y'all keep crying about wanting a good black man. But when you get us, we get thrown to the wolves. What is it that you want? Yo' baby daddy sure ain't shit from what I heard? I bet he ain't never had to deal with this bullshit like I do, right Shabria. I know his ass wasn't helping y'all out with shit. He probably had y'all using free newspaper for toilet tissue and shit. Man, fuck all that. Tyrone, man let's roll out" said Ricoe angrily and he left with Tyrone.

Shabria's face fell to the floor on that one. Ricoe had never talked down to her like that before. Shabria wondered if that was the alcohol talking or if that's how he really felt. He made it seem like she was a gold digger and she ain't like that shit at all. Neicy shook her head at all the crazy mess he was saying to her.

"Tend to that piece of shit and holla at me later. I know yo' ass is in love and shit and I get that. But I can't with him today, a'ight. I is out," said Neicy's lying ass. Shabria knew her bestie too well. Her ass had no intention of leaving because she a'int wanna miss out on a fight between them. Did somebody holla "free food?" Neicy's nosy self wasn't going nowhere. Especially, when free food and liquor was concerned. Neicy lived for drama on another woman's account of course. All her ass did was sit back down in the chair ready to see a show. They both watched Ricoe and Tyrone exchange heated words in private. But that's just how her man rolled. Ricoe Jones was private as shit. Ain't nobody know nothing about his ass and that's the way he liked it. Now for Shabria, that was a totally different story altogether. They had been messing around for two months and she still ain't no shit about his ass for real. Now, the homeless guy took the cake. But her problem wasn't so much about him showing up unannounced, it was all about her secretive ass man she done hooked up with. His ass was a lil' too flirtatious and moody for her. *I guess Mama Tawanda was right after all about that ninety day honeymoon period,* thought Shabria. She looked over at him again as the homeless man left. He went right back to grilling like ain't shit happened. Shabria decided to go over to chat with her man. It wasn't like she had something better to do. Neicy was busy talking to they girl, Trina.

Probably telling all they business and shit. Shabria ain't care because what was done was done. Ricoe was pissed off and Shabria knew it too. Something just didn't feel right no more. It was if she was losing him. Little would she expect that one day it could be true. Shabria went right over to the grill pleading and begging her man not to go. The whole time she was up in his face, he kept looking back at Neicy. Shabria tried her best to ignore it because she didn't want to cause any more trouble. It was fucked up how he kept looking at her best friend like that though. It was like his eyes were glued to hers and he refused to take them off of her and she knew it. *What else can I do,* thought Shabria.

"Bae, I did not want y'all to meet like this. Two of the closest people in my life meet and it's a disaster. Yo' ass know that I do love you and want to be with you like that? Don't make me choose between y'all! We all had too much to drink this evening. Things was said that we ain't mean to say, a'ight," cried Shabria.

A few ladies in the back was pumping her head up to be funny. Hollering, "I know that's right high yellow. Don't let Neicy disrespect yo' man like that. After he treated us all to this here BBQ for real. Her ugly ass got a nerve to be treating that man greasy like that!" hollered the nosey ass tenants. Shabria put her loving hand on his shoulder to break the ice.

Ricoe pushed her hand away because he wasn't trying to hear that shit at all. *Ain't no woman ever supposed to talk shit to a man like that,* thought Ricoe. He still turned around because he was trying to play that mess off. He knew he played a huge part in that shit, the most. "Damn, baby! You got a strong ass grip there for a petite lil' thang. Kinda manly there if you asked me. Bae is yo' ass on steroids?" laughed Ricoe.

He started tickling her like it was no tomorrow. It did feel good to bounce back so easily. Shabria laughed and tickled him right back thinking it was all good between them, but it really wasn't. Not totally, because she felt that shit. It was something in her man's eyes again and she ain't like that shit one bit. That quick, he switched up and became a man that she didn't know. Shabria started thinking about her mama's ninety-day bullshit now. *Does this fool got a multiple personality disorder too? Because I could have swore his ass was over this shit a minute ago with me.*

"Hold up, Shorty. Back the fuck off for real and don't hush me either. I don't give a fuck who hears me, a'ight! It ain't going down like that with that bitch over there, a'ight. I want this shit to work out between us now. Meaning you and me! I love yo' ass too but I ain't got to be cool with yo' girl Neicy like that too. Come on now. That is the dumbest shit to do in these circumstances. Yo' ass ain't never supposed to add no third person in our shit. I ain't in the streets but I damn sure been around the block and shit. Let that hoe stay where she is, a'ight on gawd. If yo' ass insist on it and you is forcing me to be cool with her and all that, than fuck it. That will be on you in the long run. Yo' ass ought to know better than to force a friendship between us like this. I will do that stupid shit for yo' ass," and he was dead serious about that too. Shabria ain't care as long as they ass got along. Shabria was all smiles now. She grabbed his arm like she won a prize trophy and shit.

"Yo' ass ain't trying to let me go for nothing. Even if it's for dear life, is you Shabria Reid? Sometimes that's a good and a bad thang, Sexy. I want to know just how far you is willing to go and shit. I like to test limits and shit, a'ight," winked Ricoe. The young lovers happily went back over to Neicy.

Shabria was cheesing hard for the man she loved and wasn't afraid to show it neither. *Ain't nothing like having a man on yo' arm that really wants to be with you like that. After all the ugly frogs I done kissed too. My ass deserve a to have a fucking prince all to myself,* thought Shabria. When they got over there, Ricoe did as he was ordered to do regardless of what he thought about it. He even extended his hand out to her and Neicy eagerly accepted it.

"Yo, man. You made your point, a'ight. Chill please! We all make mistakes from time to time. Just let that shit go for real. Yo' ass planned a bomb ass cookout for this whole fucking apartment complex, Cuzzo. Let's do the damn thang, a'ight. Ain't no sense in crying over spilled milk now," said Neicy as she put up her middle finger to two over the hill ladies looking all down her throat. *Like really, y'all!* They was at least thirty-five or something. "Y'all ungrateful old hoes need to turn yo' cameras the fuck off for real. If it wasn't for this power couple, y'all asses would still be swallowing oodles of noodles down and them

nasty ass sardines in a fucking can for real. Show some love for this pretty young couple, a'ight. Put some respect on they name. Yo' deejay, spin something we can all dance too," said Neicy with a big smile. Ricoe and Shabria was already kissy faced. They couldn't stay mad long and that's what Neicy was talking about. They was in the best kind of love. That toxic shit that makes yo' skin crawl. That shit that everybody wanted to be a part of. Real talk.

Ricoe was sizing her up with his slanty, scrunchy eyes. He imagined that his tongue was licking every curve of Shabria's slim-thick body. Ricoe then closed his eyes to hide his lust for the chocolate beauty in his presence. He loved that Neicy's juicy full lips and imagined what that mouf would do to him.

"Hi, I'm Ricoe Jones and it's nice to meet you, Neicy. I'll do anything in the world for my girl. I love yo' girl to death a'ight! That's the thang with new love. Yo' ass neva know what you getting yourself into or what to expect for real. I'm in it for the long haul just so yo' ass know. I ain't throwing in the towel for nothing, a'ight," said Ricoe directly.

Neicy knew a slick ass mouth when she seen it. *His ass is for the streets, periodt! I done been around and fucked a many husbands, boyfriends and baby daddies, playa. I know the fucking game. In fact, I invented that shit Ricoe,* thought Neicy to herself. Ricoe was saying shit but wasn't talking about nothing.

"A'ight, I'm down with it for my girl's sake. We is good, a'ight. Matter a fact, let's raise our cups up to congratulate new love and shit. I think a toast is due! But first I gots to tear that plate down like it ain't no tomorrow. A big girl like me can eat now." said Neicy. Ricoe and Shabria was all smiles now. The way they French kissed sent chills down Neicy's spine. That man did

love her somewhat. The way he looked at her and ran his hands through her scarlet hair was fire though. Shabria held onto him like crazy glue. *That's some black love, a'ight,* thought Neicy.

Most of the tenants had gone to they apartments and the rest was finally minding they own business. It wasn't nothing to make a spectacle about. They was on some he say she say shit. Shit happens and it was hot as fuck outside. Shabria looked up and seen that most of the apartment window's blinds was closed. Some even turned they lights off and shit. Besides, everybody in the ghetto knew that snitches get stitches. Neicy was in her feelings herself at that time. *It's something how these red-boned bitches stay winning.*

Just the other day, this hoe was rotting in the gutter for real. Bitch ain't have two pennies to rub together. How and the world is this bitch going to come up overnight before I do? Come on now, her flat, pancake ass ain't got no business with a dime like him. I can't even get a man like that to look my way if my life depended on it. I just got to do what I have to because a sista is sick and tied of being dogged out all the time! Why can't Neicy be a pillow princess sometimes, shit? Shabria light-skinned ass only got dogged out for only a lil' bit. My ass is still out here lonely and used. That's real fucked up. Her ass done survived a low-life no good ass baby daddy to wind up with a fucking Ricoe type. Oh, I am definitely jealous as fuck now! Happy, but it should have been me on his arms instead of her, thought Neicy. *Plus, the whole ghetto would forever be loyal to Ricoe because his ass done hook the projects up with food, hookah and liquor. Shit, the whole fucking block ate good. Oh, and her mans know that I want to get ate too for real! His ass done earned the black king crown as far as I'm concerned and all the other* hood *rats in that bitch,* thought Neicy.

"Now, that's what I'm talking about. That champagne life for my beautiful queen. That's what's up, you dig," and he continued to French-kiss Shabria in her mouth real nasty like. He even put his huge hands all down in her tiny, ripped shorts. "It's all good Neicy. We is family now. I'm gonna marry this chick right here one day. We ain't never going to stay mad for too long. When a man like me say he gave up on love, believe his ass. I been kicking it by myself for a minute now without any fam for real. I grew up in foster care for real," said Ricoe. Shabria was shocked because she ain't never heard that one before. Him being a poet and a chef was surprising enough and now this.

In the two months they been together, Ricoe never mentioned any of that. Shabria tried to play it off in front of her girl but it was hard to concentrate. Ricoe was digging and digging in her stuff, all while starring at Neicy and she tried to ignore it. Ricoe was just nasty and vulgar like that. *It's obvious he ain't learnt no lesson at all. His sexual flirtatious* ways get *shit started up quick*, thought Neicy. Neicy ain't know how Shabria ain't see that shit for real. Shabria felt embarrassed how he dug all in her right in front of Neicy like that.

"On some real shit, tell me how yo' ass met my girl! We is here for y'all two month anniversary and shit, right. Yo' ass is putting it all on the table, right. Leave something to the imagination, damn!" shouted Neicy. Ricoe started licking his fingers and sticking them in and out of Shabria's mouth. Her ass was into all that freaky shit. Neicy could tell that Shabria wanted to advert her attention off her man pleasuring her.

"Yeah, we got a love story alright. You should already know, Girl. I too had given up on love for a minute. I had a string of bad relationships and entanglement before this sexy, chocolate man

came into my life. Especially with my deadbeat, baby daddy, Tyrik. But all that's behind me now. I prayed about it and God finally answered my prayers. Look at God's work, Neicy," said Shabria all glowing and shit. The deejay started spinning "Beautiful" by Mary. An old head was grinning with his nosey ass. Those big ass dumbo ears could hear shit miles away. Neicy had to admit that the song fitted them beautifully. The way they bodies grinded in sync was magical and shit. *Maybe they was made for each other,* thought Neicy. *Only time can tell. Damn, I want a man like that,* thought Neicy and all the other single ladies.

Shabria felt like she was floating away in Ricoe's slanty eyes. His sweet sticky kisses felt like nectar all over her neck. His heartbeat was in alignment with hers. It was beautiful black love for the moment. They had the few people left out there grinding too. The way Ricoe led her into the grass and twirled her around was like something out of a classic movie. Both of them looked like they a'int have a care in the world to the tenants. At least for appearances sake. All Ricoe had to do was whisper in her ear to make her giggle like a schoolgirl. Ricoe did appear to be in love and he clearly wasn't afraid to show it. Shit, that man was proud as heck to be Shabria's main squeeze. All them thirsty ass thots could tell that man of hers was a bill payer, a weave sweater and a soul snatcher in bed.

"Is y'all telling me how this love shit began or naw? What the fuck is all this for? All this touchy feely shit is only cute to y'all ass. I'm in the mood for a good ass ghetto romance to get into. Do yo' ass got a friend like you for me or something like that, Ricoe? I do entanglements, situationships and side chick hoe shit, too. I accept cash app, food stamps and bus passes too. Even if you got a disabled homeboy but still looked like you. I'll

ride his ass in his wheelchair till the fucking wheels pop off," laughed Neicy. It felt good for all of them to chop it up like that. Ain't nothing like some jokes and good laughs every now and then. Shabria couldn't wait to spill the tea to her bestie! Shabria couldn't describe how it felt when Ricoe looked into her eyes like that. On that note, Ricoe started darting his tongue in and out his girl's ear all nasty like. He was looking in Neicy's face while talking nasty in Shabria's ear. Her stupid tail was in a zone so she ain't even seen it for real. Shabria turned to face him and started sucking on his ear the way her man liked it. Anything to keep him satisfied.

"So, did my future fiancée tell you how we met, Fam? It was like a needle in a haystack to find this dime piece for real. Shabria came into my life at the right time and place. I was like fuck all that love shit and here her red ass came along. I been searching for Shabria Reid my whole life! I love yo' ass, Girl,"
And he whispered something in her ear. Neicy almost shed a tear her damn self. She would have too, but now something seemed a lil' bit off with them. Way off to be precise. It was a lil' bit too rehearsed or something. Neicy wanted to know what was up with that for real.

Ricoe continued to get his finger popping on. While still eyeing Neicy like a snack. "Bria, if you want it now, let me taste you. I want to take that sweet ass up on the rooftop to have yo' ass screaming out my name, a'ight. Let these thots know how to serve up that good, good. I bet Neicy right here would eat you out too. I know she is a two-dolla thot, no doubt," and he had the nerve to continue. "No F's given. Babe, I just call them like I see them, Love. I been around and yo' girl is dying for a threesome with us. Neicy been over here entertaining you like she yo' man

and shit. I mean here you got all these guys at this BBQ and she all up in yo' face. Why though? Shabria you is pretty and slim, thick. Neicy ass just be smiling up in yo' face a lil' too much," said Ricoe. Shabria was beyond embarrassed now. It was obvious that her man had a little too much to drink. She had no clue that Ricoe couldn't hold his tongue under the influence of hard liquor. He was clearly doing too much now. It was foul and tasteless to her. *Being that nasty* and *demeaning to Neicy is just uncalled for*, thought Shabria. She felt the need to change the subject matter to the pg. version of it. All she wanted was for her new man and her best friend to get along, because they both were important in her life.

"See what had happened was. Let me stop geeking, Neicy. I just got hit with cupid's bow and arrow on social media. I was trolling on people's pages and shit. Y'all know how it is. Us ladies being nosey and liking pics and shit. I joined a couple of black dating groups and what not on Facebook because they was free. I had a lot of thirsty dms in my box. But when I say this brother right here came correct. Sis, he flipped the script, a'ight. We met right online. Facebook to be exact. Ain't that right Bae? It seems like just yesterday," said Shabria while smiling. She squeezed Ricoe's hand on the low for reassurance of things. Neicy didn't notice at first that their body language was a lil' bit off now. It was like a forced chemistry that had quickly evaporated. Ricoe shot Shabria a look to kill on that last comment though. *Oops, Love. I don't think yo' man agree with that there!* Neicy didn't know what made her do what she did out of the blue. It just felt like the right thing to do under the circumstances of course. It was truly innocent though if Ricoe was going to be in her girl's life like that. Neicy did what any bestie would do. Click on her camera to snap

a pic of the first man and lady of ghetto love.

Ricoe had an odd, sinister look on his face. Shabria was so busy sucking hickies on his neck to notice anything. Neicy laughed because it was pointless. *Like who is gonna see that shit on his black ass neck anyway.*

"Yo' ass know better than to fuck wit me like that right, Neicy? Why is yo' ass snapping a pic for? Give me that fucking phone or else!" shouted Ricoe and he grabbed her arm roughly. He started bending her fingers back causing excruciating and unnecessary pain. Neicy screamed and tried to wiggle herself free from his grip. Shabria tried to force Ricoe off her best friend.

"Bae, please stop! You is hurting her. Stop. Stop. Let her just delete it, Bae. It ain't that serious, a'ight!" yelled Shabria. At that moment, Ricoe caught himself. He realized that he had snapped and was being unnecessarily petty. He finally let up and released his grip on her. He almost sounded heartfelt and apologetic.

"Neicy, Shabria! I is sorry about that. I lost control for a second. I just don't like my photos all over Facebook and shit. Just permanently delete that shit, a'ight," and he looked scared to death about it. Shabria tried to hug him and pat him gently. She even caressed and massaged his back like he was a saint and shit. Neicy wasn't having any part of his shit. Her dude had a violent streak and she ain't like it. Ricoe lay hands on her like she stole something and what not.

"Bae, it's all good. Neicy will do that for you, a'ight. It's just bad judgement on her part. It will be deleted and will never happen again! That's all. Neicy everybody don't post things for likes and follows, a'ight. That's your thang, Sis," said Shabria relieved. Ricoe seemed to be calming down finally.

"Wayment, that shit don't sound right. How y'all meet on

Facebook then without his profile pic and info then? If yo' ass is online looking for new coochie, how is that private then? Y'all, make it make sense then," said Neicy as she shakes her head.

"Why is yo' ass so pressed for info is what I wanna know? I met her on the fucking chatline since yo' ass is so thirsty. I distinctly remember the exact day and time too! Bae, remember how I was checking for yo' ass and shit," said Ricoe with a disturbed look on his face. The way his lips was twisted up scared the shit out of Neicy. Shabria quickly responded because Ricoe forced a tight, death grip on her arm now.

Her arm turned blood red immediately. Shabria ain't never see her man act like that before. *Why is he lying about how we met because his ass know we done met up on Facebook?*

Ricoe knew he had fucked up. That Neicy just got under his skin in the worst way. That shit she did made him get hard like a mutherfucker and he loved that fire shit, too. Luckily, Shabria altered his freaky way of seeing things.

"You right, Bae! It was the chatline. I don't know what I was thinking for real. I just know that it's been the best two months of my life. I am so lucky that a man like you chose me, a'ight. Happy, happy anniversary My Love! Neicy, if you pray long and hard enough yo' ass might luck up and get a man like Ricoe! I love this man to death, a'ight," exclaimed Shabria in front of her new man. He ain't pay her red ass no attention and went all in on Neicy instead.

"Look, Sweetheart I done fucked up wit yo' ass already. I know how you ladies is. When a man fucks up, his ass gotta pay up, right? I ain't tried to go to central booking or get my pretty ass locked up tonight. I ain't gonna lie but I tend to get a lil' rough if you know what I mean. So, I tell yo' ass what, Neicy girl," said

Ricoe and he pulled out his fat ass wallet. Neicy's eyes lit up like fireworks. Ricoe's chocolate ass had bands galore and Neicy was loving that shit. Shabria started pouting and folding her hands across her chest all mad and shit. Neicy was emptying out her wallet to let him know she wanted it.

"I is a lil' low on funds, a'ight. Bri, if it's alright wit yo' ass. I like what I see. He did just fuck me up and shit. Don't be stingy now, Bestie. We is supposed to share most thangs and shit, right?" said Neicy all nasty. Shabria was done after that.

"Bae, can I holla at you in private? I must be missing something here. How is my man throwing bands at my best friend like that alright? It was a fucking mistake, Ricoe? Why can't yo' ass respect yo' woman by just apologizing and shit? You is doing too much. Her ass cuts up and yo' dumb ass is doing the most, Einstein! And for yo' ass, Neicy fuck no! I ain't sharing my man's wallet with no other chick out here, a'ight! The only other girl is my baby, Ti'aja," yelled Shabria. Neicy sucked her lips and teeth in like whatever hoe! Her man was spassing and she was accepting and that was that.

"Look, where I is from that's how we handle thangs. Shabria, a'ight. It costs big time when anybody fucks up. To keep small shit from escalating into something big and that's it. The last I checked Bae; this was my shit, right? As long as I'm taking care of home, what the fuck is yo' problem then? Ain't no woman controlling my wallet unless I want them to. Fix yo' face all scrunched up and shit. Don't be so stingy! This money ain't hurting you and yours! The home front is already taken care of and shit! Ain't Neicy yo' girl? Bae, I owe her and she can use the hush money. What if the police was to come, huh? I done made my mind up. Get over it!" yelled Ricoe. ***Now this is some fucked up***

shit, thought Shabria to herself. But what else could she do or say about it? Ricoe handed Neicy the money and she stuffed it in her bra. Her ass had the nerve to lean all the way down so he could see inside her bra. Ricoe started smiling hard as shit at her huge erect nipples.

"I'm just going to leave that shit alone for right now. It's getting late and I need to get the kids in soon. Mostly, everybody is gone anyways. Neicy, don't yo' ass got somebody to do in the backseat?" asked Shabria sarcastically. Neicy shrugged her shoulders and sat back in the folding chairs.

"No, no and no! I ain't leaving till y'all spill the tea for real. I gots all night, Sis! I still ain't get the full unedited scoop yet. I want to hear the story about how Shabria really met Ricoe, a'ight. I am a sucker for them love stories and a Sis is feeling good tonight too. A hood love story is just what I need. I got paper in my wallet to go shopping and shit. I ate and drank good and I'm enjoying myself. All I want to know respectfully is how y'all met. Give me couple goals and shit, bestie. Ain't nothing wrong with that is it? I get goosebumps when it comes to that toxic love. Shabria, yo' ass should know me by now," said Neicy. Shabria wasn't in the mood for that crap. *Her disrespectful ass done went through my man's wallet and then got the nerve to try to kick it with me of all people. Her ass is a lil' too pressed about how I met my man*, thought Shabria. Ricoe took over their convo because he was loving the attention. He put his muscular arms around his girl's tiny waist to calm her jealous ass down. He wanted to get to know Neicy's ass too. He was blushing hard as hell too. That was Neicy's cue to go on. *Fuck Shabria's snobby lil' ass*, thought Neicy. Her man was paying her some attention so she was all for it.

"Get the fuck outta hear, y'all. Cuzzo and yo' ass is a poet, too. If you write a poem about y'all shit that will be fire and lit for the people! Just don't fuck it up with no flying unicorns and shit. Us ratchet girls don't like that imaginary shit. Keep yo' shit straight gutta and ratchet! Ain't nobody wanna hear about no man riding in on no white horse and shit. We is in the hood. Give us a story about the man putting mousetraps behind the refrigerator and shit. A man that knows where the quality weed is at for real. We wanna hear about riding his ass like a cowgirl and shit. Fuck a horse! Get gritty and raw with it, y'all." Neicy was clearly a lil' too much into it.

"Neicy. What kind of fools is yo' ass dealing with? I don't want no man laying down no traps and shit. His ass better be the fucking exterminator and maintenance man up in my crib for real," laughed Shabria. She went along with that crazy ass Neicy because she felt sorry for her pitiful ass. Besides, it wasn't no harm in talking because at the end of it, he was going home with her anyway. *It's sad how some ladies lower they standards just to have a man around. Neicy ass is just ghetto and not walking in her purpose at all,* thought Shabria. Neicy continued as if she was the only person outside and shit.

"Smack a few hoes when they is foul and disrespectful, a'ight Playa! Do some on the run crime spree and shit. Go on the run together toxic love shit, a'ight," said Neicy with wild open eyes.

Shabria thought her ass was hilarious with it for real. The hoe obviously had too much time on her hand. *Ain't no way in hell I'd be worrying about the next chick like that,* thought Shabria. *Hoes be needing a life or something to do for real.*

"Neicy Girl, sorry to bust yo' bubble. But uh, we ain't rolling like that, a'ight. A lil' bit ghetto and that's just about it. I is his

ride or die don't get me wrong. But I am too fucking pretty to be in jail! The only crime I'd commit is a crime of illicit passion for my man. Ricoe can handcuff me for life and throw away the only key, real talk. Ain't nothing wrong about being tied up and blindfolded though. I lives for that freak nasty shit. Sorry Bae, I had to throw in some nasty shit to hold my girl's interest. Look at her ass drooling over there and shit. What I tell you, Bae?" said Shabria with a sexy smirk on her face.

"Oh, I likes it's right on the money. If it ain't freak nasty, I don't want it. Keep going! Don't stop now!" whispered Neicy. The alcohol was starting to affect her ears. To her, Shabria's voice had n a sexy, sultry tone to it. Shabria looked at her man and he was enjoying their convos. Feeling naughty, Shabria put her hands down his gray sweats. He was feeling it alright, gotdamn.

"As far as a threesome, I would be down if my man wants one. If I can't please my man or fulfill his sexual fantasies than why is he claiming me, right? But not no fucking bestie of mine though. Ain't just any old chick deserving of that shit. He ain't shy about going down, out and beyond. We pleases each other. Ricoe can eat it for days, Girl. That huge..." said Shabria and she covered her mouth. It was obvious that she was still tipsy because her yellow ass was spilling tea, coffee and cocoa now. It was fire, too. It was blowing both Ricoe's heads up now. Neicy was smiling at the images of the lovers getting real nasty, nasty. She was ready to eat both of them up.

"Bae, if yo' ass is going to tell it like it is, don't leave the gooey wet stuff out. Tell yo' bestie how I like pouring strawberry syrup down the crack of yo' sweet ass and licking it then. I like sticking marshmallows in every hole and shit, too. I mesmerize and be hypnotic when it comes to the freaky shit, Neicy. I have you

doing thangs that yo' ass could have never imagined and shit. Ain't that right, Bae?" said his horny ass. Ricoe had a nerve to wink at Neicy and stick out a wiggly tongue. Neicy was so hot and wet that she felt faint. She was beyond hot and bothered now. This man had dropped a couple of bands on her ass and had the audacity to be seducing her mind too. *With his fine, chocolate ass self.*

"Unfortunately, I am a one woman man Neicy. I like to tease you but that is as far as my tongue will go."

"I can't put my mouth on everybody, you feel me. My 12-inches only can coat Shabria's throat, a'ight," said Ricoe, the soul snatcher.

The nasty freak had the nerve to masturbate right in front of her. He had his hands down his pants going to town. "If I wanted her too Neicy, Shabria would give me some head right in front of you. I know you would too, nasty Neicy. Let me stop fucking with yo' ass before yo' ass eat through my girl's panties, right in broad daylight," said Ricoe and he started laughing sadistically. Ain't none of them see anything wrong with a lil' adult, grown fun. Laughing ain't never hurt nobody. Shabria all hot and horny felt the need to keep up with they sexual display. She took his hands out his boxers and sucked and licked his cream off. Neicy was done because she was having multiple orgasms back to back.

"I can't with y'all nasty asses! All I needed to know was how y'all met for real. It's still some kids nearby, damn! Somebody's granny is right over there, nasty ass!" said Neicy.

"I know one thang though. Ricoe yo' nasty ass hands don't need to be grilling nobody's food like that. Ain't no telling where that mouth been or those nasty ass hands of yours now. I can't lie but I'm feeling y'all now. That's that fire love that we all need up in our life. Y'alls thang is toxic as shit and I like it a lot! But unless, y'all giving me a threesome please stop! Y'all ass don't wanna know what my mouth is willing to do, a'ight! Don't go there! My girl Shabria done lucked up and found herself a beast on that fucking chatline for real! Was it on the sexual encounter's category or some BSDM type of freaky shit? Inquiring minds like mines wants to know, feel me. Which chatline? Black Hotties or Black Love? Put a sista down on it, ASAP!" said Neicy all excited.

Ricoe and Shabria couldn't help but to smile and blush. They felt like Porn Stars and shit now. *Maybe that only fans shit might do us some good. I see how my girl is over there eating it up. Some freaky people probably do get off on watching other couples' fuck. If either of our ass get out of work or laid off, it's on. Money is money, especially when yo'* ass is doing something *yo' ass like,* thought Shabria. On God, Neicy thought they was so cute together. Ricoe started strutting like a proud peacock now.

"Oh, I got this my Queen. None of those actually, Neicy. We met on the Black Professionals Chatline and shit. Right here in Maryland. Being a sexy, chocolate and highly intellectual man, I made the cut! It was time for me to search for my Queen, Shabria. A beautiful, transparent woman of substance and value and purpose. I found that and more in this woman right here!" said Ricoe and he started kissing all over Shabria again. Shabria couldn't help but to giggle and to return her man's advances back.

Blushing hard, Shabria decided to tap in on her man's story. Even though that was not how it went at all. Shabria figured that since he claimed to be a poet that he must loved making up vivid

stories for no reason.

"Neicy, I know what you is thinking, Sis. How I get on the chatline then with my ghetto ass, right? I know you and Trina crack slick behind my back and shit. Y'all be like Shabria been doing hair her whole life and it still ain't shit. My ass can't braid or flat iron at all. The glue be showing real big in my tracks and shit. Well Boo, my man fell in love with my potential of being a bomb ass beautician. He know that I am destined to do bigger and better thangs with my life. I still got time, Neicy. I ain't reach thirty yet."

"I am just humble and patient at this point in my life. I am a good transparent person with a loving heart, that's all. My man see's and supports all my goals and ambitions. That's what attracted me to him. We chopped it up via text and facetime. It was words at first sight for me. I mean we would talk till sun up to sundown for real. When you meet that special someone that love right there is magical. Even at only two months messing around with each other. When yo' ass know, you'll know," cried Shabria with real genuine tears of joy.

Neicy was in awe, real shit. The way Ricoe looked at her like he'd hit the jackpot on that one. *It's real nice to see a love like that so up close and personal*, thought Neicy. It was really like nothing she'd ever seen on reality tv and movies. Even those classic black and white movies ain't have nothing on them. It was a beautiful thang to see a decent black man cherishing a black woman for a change. Social media had the single life doomed and pitiful. All the singles they knew was bitter, hurt and savage. They wanted revenge on any person that crossed their path because of what the person did to them before they came into the picure. It was sad because the majority was just petty and shitty as hell. Neicy

and a few others all seemed to believe that Shabria had a good thang. Her man was a flirt but who's wasn't thought Neicy. They were holding hands when Ricoe tapped back in.

"Well, Neicy, that's all the mushy shit. But it wasn't all peaches and cream for me. When I slid in, she was giving me a hard way to go. I mean I got that she was broken down and hurt. My baby had years of being used, abused and cheated on before me. Her crown was falling off when I was trying to holla at her pretty ass," said Ricoe being extra again.

"It was my job to fix her crown and that wasn't easy for me at all. I had a hard time convincing her that all men ain't the same. Ricoe Jones is that one in a million and I hope she never forgets that, regardless of what happens next. Bria had some serious trust issues going on alright. As a man of God, I stayed upfront and transparent about everythang in my life the whole time. I ain't got nothing to hide. My woman knows everything about me. How else should a spiritual man court a woman like her?" said Ricoe lying through his teeth. *He is definitely a poet with that imagination of his*, thought Shabria.

The reality was far from the truth now that she thought about it. Ricoe ain't really say shit about himself. Just that he was a black professional and that he lived in West Baltimore. But that wasn't saying shit really. Being a poet and a chef was new news to her. To this day, she ain't never know what her new boo did for a living for real. His profile only stated black professional now that she thought about it. She ain't never even been invited to his crib in all that time. All she knew was that her new man made boo-hoo money at something, but what though? Ricoe kept stacks of bands on him at all times. His ass dressed as sharp as a razor. He stayed jeweled up while rocking Dolce and

Gabana, Gucci and Givenchy tailored suits like a mutherfucker. His whips looked like that were dripping diamonds and what not. He stayed drenched in sparkling bling, bling jewelry. That man was drowning in that luxurious shit for real. Today, his sexy ass switched up and got low-key street like the thugs on the corner. Shabria couldn't take his imagination no more. That shit was crazy. Shabria didn't know whether to hug him or pluck him upside the head for real.

"Bae, was all that even necessary. You make it seem like my life was over before I met yo' ass. I was never that bad off now. So, please stop exaggerating every damn thang! I admit that I was in a really bad place at that time but I wasn't dying now. You is being extra with all that. I felt down and worthless but that was on me. I felt ugly till you reminded me that I am still pretty, Bae. Yo' sweet Hershey bar ass came and did the damn thang. Yo' ass swept me off my feet. Ricoe, I thank you for teaching me how to love again. I was on some all men ain't shit jazz for a minute," said Shabria sincerely.

Shabria continued with real sincere tears in her eyes. Neicy felt that too because that right there hit close to home for her. Ain't nothing worser than getting dumped repeatedly, ghosted or played. Shit, her and Shabria was almost damaged for life because of it. Those painful bruises and scars were the hardest to heal. That shit burns every time yo' ass is naked in the shower. Yo' ass will cry and question yo' existence in that man's life for real. What is yo' ass doing wrong to keep on being treated like shit? The cheating was the ultimate betrayal for the both of them. You spend countless nights up in bed worrying about his other woman for real.

Even in her hoeish ways, Neicy still had feelings. She had her days too. Being the side chick and the mistress was catching up with her now. The attached guys would be on their knees between her talking about their girl. Always she ain't doing this or that dumb shit. *Like how is going down on me going to change* that, thought Neicy? As a woman she wanted to know what their significant other had over her ass. All the men she fucked went back home to they main girl after. It was always like what do they have that I don't type of thang for her. *Why is my ass not worth wifing up, the fuck?*

Neicy cried worrying to death about what she was lacking in sex a many of nights for real. Even knowing that the man was never yours to begin with fucked her head up. Neicy took a huge L every time they crept out of her squeaking bed, real shit. The life of a thot was not as glamorous as kept women thought it was for real. It was always some bullshit about what the main chick wasn't doing in the bed. *At the end of the day, they was all just lying, cheating dogs to her anyways.*

Now, the besties had a real dilemma between them, a whole man. Not just any man but the love of her best friend's life, Ricoe Jones. *It that ain't gonna go down to well,* thought Neicy. Ricoe caught the ladies looking all down and shit and wanted to play hero and shit to his advantage. It wasn't no funeral so he thought he'd bring the two ladies in his life back to life.

"What's with the sad, long faces huh? Life moves on. Shit happens to the best of us. Yo' ass is going to win some and lose some and that's life. Put a band aid on that shit and keep it moving for real. Hold yo' crowns up cause now yo' ass is a part of Ricoe's world. Let the past go! I done planned this bomb ass cookout too. I don't know nobody in these projects for real. Look at dude over there. I call him Cuzzo and don't even know that man like that. When I walked up on a scene back in the day, I got mad respect on gawd. I'm talking about free food, free pussy and then some every day. They be throwing mad cash at me too. When Ricoe Jones is in town it's raining dolla's. Believe that, cause its real shit. Shabria, don't go looking at me all crazy. This was before I even met you, now," said Ricoe with his conceited ass. Dark chocolate thought he was the shit. Shabria and Neicy looked like they were thinking the same things. Shabria's instincts told her to take it there with her man and she did.

"But Bae, that would have been about two months ago then. Where is all them hoes now? The way yo' ass sling wood I know they ain't cutting yo' ass off that easily. In fact, them thots is probably still checking for you, Ricoe! I know they is doing everythang and anything to get yo' ass back. I ain't stupid now," and she was dead serious about it too.

"Man whateva! Shabria is right on point. I know that bitches stay thirsty for dick that they can't have or keep. You is lying on that, Bruh. You is trying to tell us that they is a'ight getting cut off and shit. See, that's some old bullshit right there cause I know me. I am still chasing after the dogs that screwed me over and dipped currently. So, ain't no way them chicks is out the picture, Man. You ain't fooling nobody but Shabria's dumb tail," yelled Neicy. They had been drinking and carrying on all evening and all they shit was getting old. Ricoe was sick and tied of the ladies trashing him for no reason. He got up and was ready to leave before he said or did something that he would regret. Shabria all hyped up wasn't trying to let that shit go at all though.

"I don't know for real Ricoe. Yo' ass got a whole man's cave over west that I ain't even seent yet for real. Just cause I got the password to unlock yo' phone don't mean shit really. It was cute

how we recorded a voicemail greeting together for yo' phone and shit. My pretty face is on yo' screensaver and locked screen. But what the fuck, Bae? Yo' ass is still probably out there behind my back. Nowadays, you can't put shit past nobody for real," cried Shabria and now she was just pissy drunk.

"I might as well carry my black ass back over west then for all this unnecessary shit. I'm going to pay cuzzo over there to shut this shut down for me." That hit close to home.

"His ass should do it for free with his little crumb snatcher ass, a'ight," said Ricoe as he walked over to kiss his girl a see you later. Shabria took a smooch on the cheek because that was all she thought she deserved. All night she had been treating her man greasy out of insecurities. What was more fucked up was her letting Neicy nasty ass get into her head. She understood why them old cougars said not to take relationship advice from yo' single, jealous girlfriends. Too late. Shabria could tell by his eyes that he was really hurt. Her and Neicy literally ripped the man apart. So, she did what any woman in her right mind would do.

"Bae, don't leave me mad like this, please. I know I done fucked up our first BBQ and shit. I'm fucking toxic, sexy! I know my yellow ass is difficult to love and deal with. Won't you come on over after I bathe and put my kids too sleep, a'ight. Let's try to have a good night tonight, Babe. Neicy, can you excuse us so we can talk in private please and thank-you, pleaded Shabria.

For some reason, Neicy could not move or speak. Seeing the power couple fuck up and then get back together was killing her for real. She low-key ain't want they asses to go back to being lovey dovey again. Neicy wanted to see them fight, yell and curse each other out and shit. *It ain't fair to go home again to an empty*

bed like that, thought Neicy. *Why should I anyways? Her sweet eye candy ain't nothing but a fuck boy on the low. His ass is curving his girl right in front of her face like a male thot. Ricoe done let it be known that he wants to fuck me and taste me!. That sultry look in his eyes done let me know that he wants me to ride his face, too. It was wrong but hey. Why can't ride or die besties share every thang like they do in books and shit*, thought Neicy's trifling ass.

If that ain't low down dirty, I don't know what is then. Neicy decided to stay in her front row seat to see the show. *Fuck they relationship*, thought Neicy. *A bitch like me is trying to change that man's status to a complicated entanglement*, thought Neicy.

Ricoe longed to be in his girl's arms but the vibe was all screwed up. He was tied of tiptoeing around her kids and shit. He always had to sneak in when they ass was asleep and shit. Their sex was whack at her crib because they ass always had to be real quiet and shit. Shabria couldn't even scream out his name and shit. In the middle of the night, his black ass had to creep out like a thief in the night type of crazy shit. Ricoe held his woman sadly because here was another night of the same bullshit.

"I gotta love my toxic chick, right. But tonight, I'm going back to my crib. This has been one fucked up day. Toxic as fuck but I love that shit. Just hit me up in the morning, a'ight. We can take the kids to IHOP or something for breakfast. It's really whatever yo' ass want to do for real. I just need to get the fuck out of here. I'm still hella tipsy and yo' girl is looking all down my throat and shit. I'm a thug and feel uncomfortable in this situation. Yo' ass should respect me as yo' man and let me go on about my business tonight, for real, a'ight," pleaded Ricoe.

Shabria was caught in a dilemma though. She still didn't want her kids to see Mr. Ricoe in her bed. On the other hand, she didn't want Neicy's nasty ass in her man's bed either. Because drunk or not, his black ass was a lil' too flirtatious with her best friend. She knew for a fact that her man was horny as fuck too. *He is definitely gonna want some coochie from somebody tonight,* thought Shabria.

That old nasty thang would have fucked my new man silly, no doubt. Neicy was over there with a tight face feeling betrayed and shit. She figured if her best friend's man wanted to hit, he better cut the red bone off. It ain't look like that was happening so she purposely cut in and provided her two cents. Neicy figured starting an argument between them would get her ass ate. Her bold ass walked right up to them and spit fire for real.

"Bria, his ass is playing yo' ass for a dummy. His ass is still for the streets, a'ight. If he is yo' man he is supposed to go home with you. Ain't nothing happen that bad tonight for his sneaky ass to dip out on yo' ass like that. Don't be no fool Sis! He is a fucking thot and I know that. That man ain't wearing no ring means his ass is single and ready to mingle. If he can't stay the night Sis, kick his black ass to the curb, a'ight!" yelled Neicy while attempting to cause static and trouble between the couple. Her interference had been working in her favor all this time. *Her man already done dropped two-thousand on her for some coochie as it is. His ass thought he was slick talking about it is fucking hush money. Ok, what man does that huh,* thought Neicy? Shabria caught on to her girl's schemes and read that bitch her rights. Shabria was ready to fuck her girl up of that stupid shit for real. She decided not to because she ain't need no more bad blood between them. That would gave her full ammunition to fuck her man then. Shabria decided to come across as a lady instead. Not just any lady but Ricoe Jone's main lady.

"Thanks Sis! I appreciate you having my back and all but we got this. My man is a lil' flirtatious but that's it. I just don't think he would cross the line on me like that. Ain't that right Bae? Yo' ass respect boundaries, right?"

"After all that personal shit, I done told yo' ass, I know yo' ass wouldn't be that crazy! If so, I is doing a Loraina Bobbet on yo' shit for real. I rather yo' ass walk away than to cheat on me and betray my trust," said Shabria. Ricoe just stood there looking crazy. He ain't know what to say to that shit at all. He started scratching his beard and looking down on the ground. Neicy took advantage of that shit fast as a heartbeat.

"See, what I tell yo' red ass! He ain't got shit to say because I'm telling the truth, Sis. It's in his eyes. His ass can't even look and think straight now. I should know because we is alike in some ways. I already done made a name for myself so I don't fucking care no more. I been freaking and hoeing so long that I can spot they asses out now. I crave another woman's supposedly faithful dick. It's a sickness and an addiction now. I can't help myself. The kind that ain't mine and I got to creep and shit for it. I want it and it is a lot of other thirsty hoes out here like me too. Y'all stay coming after the sidepieces when yo' man needs to come correct first. Look at his fine, rich ass. I'm telling yo' ass he ain't gonna be able to hold out like that, Shabria. Yo' ass is in love and I get that. Yo' ass ain't got to listen to the shit that I got to say. Just so yo' ass know, Ricoe, Remy or whateva yo' name is. Ain't no dick golden enough to tear me and my bestie apart, Sir. So, you best to be sticking all 12 inches up in my girl right here, a'ight or else," lied Neicy. Shabria ain't know what was up but her man did. *His girl ain't never been about that life. Shabria clearly ain't ready*, thought Neicy. "Y'all need some help cleaning up. It's getting late as fuck for real. A lot of people done left already anyway," said Neicy. Ricoe was relieved how Neicy changed the subject to distract his girl. He ain't want to answer his girl because he ain't have shit to say for real.

Neicy's ratchet ass was on point with all her shit. Shabria had a lot on her plate as it was too. She decided to leave that convo alone for the time being. It was definitely going to come back up. His black ass had a lot of explaining to do. His sneaky ass was making up jobs and shit. A fucking hobo was acting strange earlier. *Don't let my ass find out that he is not the man his ass claim to be,* thought Shabria. *I'm going to fry that ass coal the fuck black if he is pulling my leg.*

"Yeah, we can use your help, Neicy Girl. Ain't that right Babe? Look at all that shit over there, y'all. These greedy ass section eight tenant's ain't want to be cleaning up shit for real. We is got trash bags tied to every other chair and they lazy ass still ain't give a fuck about us! I took a risk hosting on somebody else's rental property for they asses and this is what I get in return. This don't make no fucking sense! I hate it here for real. Our lease prohibits shit like this!" yelled Shabria and she started picking up trash from the grass.

"I say fuck the landlord and HUD for real. These poor tenants is trapped and caged like prisoners in this shit hole. Ain't no way that the city should be paying they ass no subsidized check every month for this crap. The city of Baltimore got all this money and this is the best they can do. Get the fuck out of here, Housing Authority! I say throw this whole apartment complex in the trash for real," said Ricoe as he started folding chairs.

Shabria started cheesing again when it came to her mans. Neicy was sick of her shit and that fucked up hairdo. Her shit was played out. *Ain't no way that old ass hairdo is still popping in 2021,* thought Neicy. Neicy wondered how she even got a man as fine as Ricoe. *His ass must just be into redbones because that bitch look like a duck wit a mop on her head."*

Neicy laughed to herself. Her known jealously for they situationship was starting to kick in again. Neicy rolled her eyes and sucked in her teeth behind her besties back of course.

"That's my mans right here. He is always for the people. I dig that, Sexy. We got to do what we got to do sometimes that's all. This is the most decent projects to accept vouchers in East Baltimore for real. Where else is we supposed to go? This is the only rent that my ass can afford with two babies to take care of. I ain't raising my kids in no fucking Murphy Homes!" said Shabria as she was tying up trash bags.

"Ain't nothing but crackheads and trap houses out that bitch now, I heard. Look my son, Tyrik got to grow up in these Baltimore streets and shit. I try but it's hard as fuck trying to do all this shit by yo' damn self for real. He's just eight and my baby girl, Ti'aja is six going on sixteen. They punk ass, snitch ass daddy ain't in they life but I is. I did what I had to do to raise my kids, y'all. I wasn't letting CPS cop my babies like Pebbles did. It was crazy because her ass got a check for all five kids. I'm like how yo' ass not going to have money for pampers and milk? Just how? It ain't my job to buy that hoe's pampers and shit, but I did. I'm the type of chick that don't want to see nobody starve or ass out. Me and my mans is like two peas in a pod and shit. His ass doing charity work for these ungrateful ass tenants as we speak. Pebbles got money to party in them streets though. The bitch even got food stamps and WIC, y'all. Unfit muva's like that make my blood boil for real. I ain't got no sympathy for her ass at all.

Pebbles is just trifling for real!" shouted Shabria and she was almost done cleaning her section.

Ricoe was cleaning up suspiciously like he had something to say. Shabria noticed that her man wasn't as happy as before. Neicy was on the other side chatting it up with some dude so it was perfect timing to check in with her mans. When she walked up on him, he appeared to be giving her the cold shoulder. *Now, what's wrong with his ass,* thought Shabria?

"Bae is you staying over tonight. Just wait in yo' car till my kids is sleep and I'll let you in quietly. What's wrong Bae? Is it the homeless guy or is Neicy starting shit again?" said Shabria while trying to kiss him but he pulled back instead.

"It ain't you, it's me. That lil' comment about single muva's was real fucked up. I was raised by a single woman; my grandma and she raised all my six brothers and sisters by herself. Yo' ass need to stop talking shit about people yo' ass don't even know like that for real. Yo' ass got a lot of shit with you. Talking shit and fucking up my mood and shit. I'm addicted to toxic shit but uh you is a bit much," snapped Ricoe.

He ain't saying shit his self, thought Shabria. *His ass is still fucking lying for no reason. His sneaky black ass is starting to get on my nerves for real. One minute is this and the next fucking second, it's that. Which the fuck is it Bro? Get yo' lies straight fool,* thought Shabria. *Ricoe ass stay doing the most* and *that shit is irritating. But I still love it!* Shabria walked over and grabbed Ricoe from behind. She wrapped her arms around him to make him smile. Once he smiled that gave her the greenlight to explore his eagerness. Shabria put both hands down his boxers and whispered in his ear. He was wiping off the grill when her turned around to face her.

"Bae, is you spending the night. Once the babies is sleep, it's on. Let me get them unwinded and I is all yours. Anything goes tonight, a'ight Mr. BBQ Chef," purred Shabria in his ear. Ricoe removed her hands.

His eyes darted everywhere but, in her eyes, directly. He knew it was going to be trash and had other thangs on his mind.

"What's wrong Bae? All I need is two hours tops and it's on!" pleaded Shabria. He had his eyes on that fast ass Neicy all night and still did. Everything was cleaned up and the trash was gone. Only two tenants was left and they was minding they business and smoking a blunt by the gate. The only trash that was left was Neicy who was ready to do her thot shit thang as usual. At every outing, her ass went home with somebody's man and tonight her man was the last man standing.

"Naw, can't do that shit tonight! I ain't hiding in no mutherfucking closet till' yo' kids go to sleep no more. How the fuck that look? A grown ass man playing hide and seek in his girl's closet, Shabria? I is getting tied of that ole' bullshit now! I want to wake up in our bed and hold yo' ass in my arms real bad. You just don't know!" he shouted. Shabria saw the way he was eying her bestie up and got all up in his ass for it.

"At least, I invite yo' black ass over. I can't say the same for yo' ass though. It's been two fucking months and I still don't know where yo' ass live for real, Ricoe. Besides, you know the deal at home! I got two fucking babies at home, Ricoe. As long as you getting some fool, where and what time shouldn't even matter for real" she shouted back at him. Ricoe shook his head because his girl ain't have no clue. *Ain't no man out here got to deal wit no fucking package deal in 2021*, thought Ricoe. He was tied as shit and wanted to be serviced like a fucking king for the night. He was in the mood to get freak nasty and Shabria was not down. *Why the fuck should I care about her kids*, thought Ricoe?

"See, that's the fucking problem! Yo' ass ain't got no babies at home, Shabria. Yo' ass got two kids that should be sleeping they lil' asses in they own bed and shit." That had been bugging him for a minute.

"Make they ass go in they own room and leave the adults the fuck alone for real. Tell them to bathe they asses themselves and please yo' man, a'ight! I got fucked over two times already and I ain't for that shit no more. If you can't accommodate yo' man than fuck it. I am going back to my own crib tonight!" yelled Ricoe. That was exactly what nasty Neicy wanted to hear. Her nosey ass been peeping they convo the whole time. Shabria looked over at her ass smiling and licking her lips. Shabria just ignored that bitch because Neicy wasn't the problem her man was.

"A'ight, I can do that shit. But only for tonight because of my situation. Don't act like yo' ass ain't know that upfront! Yo' ass got to work with a sista, a'ight. I can just bring yo' ass in my apartment just like that. Let me handle my home first. I got to come correct with them first. That's the least I can do. And they is my babies cause I had them. Yo' ass is child free, so yo' ass don't understand Ricoe," cried Shabria. Neicy was over there entertaining two dudes when she heard Shabria crying. Neicy bold ass walked right into it like what. Neicy looked right at her best friends' man at that.

"I need a lil' favor, y'all. I need a good ride tonight. Bria, is it okay if yo' man drives me. I mean we is girls and look out for each other and shit," said her nasty ass. Ricoe was blushing and blushing so bad he had to turn his fucking head away. He had a tough decision. Deal with his girl's shit with her two kids or fuck a sexy, phat ass thot. He loved his girl to death but temptation was the devil. He desired that Neicy though.

It was just something about her for me. Ricoe had done already made his mind up to tap that ass. It was just a matter of how soon for his no good ass.

"Neicy, he can't because he wants me to sit on his face all night. Use that money he donated to yo' ass to catch a fucking hack, a'ight. Find some other stupid bitch's man to take yo' ass home and holla at me in the afternoon, a'ight," said Shabria and she forced her tongue in Ricoe's mouth. His sneaky ass accepted her mouth while winking at Neicy.

"Damn, Bae! Yo' ass go hard for my ass, don't you? This yo' mutherfucking girl. Neicy, as yo' ass can see I can't fuck with yo' ass *tonight*. As a gentleman it's my job to drop you off. Ain't no man going to let a lady be in these streets alone at night. As far as tonight, it is what it is, a'ight. Have yourself a beautiful night, a'ight" and he walked away before his excitement in his pants showed otherwise. Neicy sucked her teeth and rolled her eyes. *This light-skin bitch think her ass got one up over me, huh. His ass going to be eating for two. Believe that, thought,* Neicy.

"Okay Girl. I hear that. I will definitely holla at yo' ass in the afternoon, a'ight. Have yourself a goodnight too and make the best of yo' situation, a'ight," lied Neicy.

"Oh, *we will* and yo' ass can take that to the bank. Thanks for being concerned bout our shit though, Sis. We been girls since diapers to periods, right. I appreciate yo' ass coming out to celebrate me and my mans two-month anniversary and shit. What is a girl to do without her bestie, huh?" said Shabria with a smirk on her face. "Yo' ass is right about that, Girl! I'd give yo' ass the

shirt of my back if yo' ass needs it. What is mines is yo' ass too? Don't forget that shit red-bone. We is girls through thick and thin."

Chapter 2: Wifey Material"

Shabria grabbed the sheets to cover her naked body. The bed was sticky from whipped cream, hot fudge and strawberry syrup. Her man was nasty as fuck in her bedroom last night. Ricoe even turned her out to be freak nasty like a Porn Star. Shabria was glad her babies was tied out or her man wasn't getting no ass last night. They little asses got in bed real early for the first time ever. Shabria wiggled her nose because something smelled delicious. It smelled like maple bacon, cheesy scrambled eggs and buttered grits. "Oh, hell no! Is his fine chocolate ass fixing seasoned home fries in my crib, too?" said Shabria out loud. *Oh, his ass is spoiling the shit outta me, ain't he*, thought Shabria to herself. Before she even had a chance to wipe the crusty crumbs out her eyes, her man was standing in front of her bucket naked and shit in her apron. Her king was even holding a tray of all that good ass breakfast food for her. Decked out with fresh squeezed orange juice too. *Now how many women can top that*, thought. Shabria.

"Good morning, Reds! Grand Rising, my Queen. Yo' man done made some bomb ass breakfast in bed like a boss! Give me some suga, Sexy," and he smiled while trying to kiss her in the mouth. Shabria made a face like eel, that shit is nasty and gross as fuck. Ricoe started smiling and shaking his head.

"My mouth, Bae! How bout yo' ass? The way yo' ass was eating my butthole last night! I still got yo' juices in my beard and what? Bria, this is luv right chere. That grown ass luv that will make you cum for hours, my love. This time, she let him stick his tongue all inside that mouth of hers.

"It's good. But do yo' ass gotta be breathing coochie breath all over my food though? I got extra toothbrushes in the closet and shit. Babe, is my babies still asleep?"

Shabria sure did hope so because he sure as hell was confidently strutting around with his ass cheeks out and shit. Her little ass apron was barely covering his long ass dick. *I know his ass know better than that*, thought Shabria. He had the nerve to be smiling and shit.

"Nah, I already done made them blueberry pancakes and fresh peach smoothies for they breakfast. I is a man of all trades, you dig. They is good, love! I got you," said Ricoe. Shabria was about to vomit thinking about his nasty ass hands feeding her babies like that.

"What's wrong, Bae? This is what yo' ass wanted, right? Yo' yellow ass begged me a hundred times when you was sitting on my face! Ooh, Zaddy. Move in wit mama! Ooh, Zaddy, please don't stop! Yo' ass remember all that crying and shit, right? Yo' man is moving the fuck in, a'ight! We is going to be the perfect family and shit, a'ight!" and he was dead serious about that shit, too. *Oh damn! I done fucked up big time,* thought Shabria to herself. She stopped eating and put the tray down real fast.

"Wayment, wayment now! I really said that shit. We ain't even had the *talk* yet though. I ain't no childless bitch in this crib, Bae. My babies is here with my ass! I'm glad we got it in when we did. But it ain't always gonna be like that for real, playa! We got lucky that time," said Shabria in shock.

"Fuck, how the shit was before, a'ight! It is a man around this bitch now and I is the stepdaddy! I been paying the bills in this crib, right. I is supposed to lay my fucking head here, don't you think? Yo' ass ain't got shit to say when I'm eating between them legs though, right? I ain't gotta a problem doing that. All I ask is that yo' ass submit, stay nasty and be *wifey material* and that's it. That ain't too much to ask for, is it? "Keep that shit clean, sweet and tight for Zaddy, a'ight. Keep my belly full and give Zaddy that bomb azz head every night and I is good. That is if yo' ass don't want me going back to the streets. I is coming home faithfully to my woman every night on gawd! If I'm coming home to just one woman, what the fuck is the problem then? Shabria?" asked Ricoe with an attitude. He was pissed after putting in all that work. *Her ass is still not responding the way she ought to and shit,* thought Ricoe to himself. His temper was rising among other thangs. *This hood luv ain't no fucking joke,* thought Shabria. Ricoe felt the need to get some things off his chest that would lead to a thot laying under it.

"We please each other in this bitch, right? I should be in charge around here! In every crib a black man is supposed to be running shit, Bria. That's the way it is, Bae! Yo' ass is real lucky to have whipped a good ass brutha like me. I is hooked like a mutherfucker now. Got me cooking and singing and shit early in the morn. A thug ain't posed to be buying roses and sharing they passcode with just any old' broad. My ass is hooked and I am loving that shit for real," said Ricoe as he started dancing and singing in her bedroom.

Shabria nodded yes, but that shit was still erky to her. She ain't like that shit like that. Shabria grew up with her mama being head of household for real and she followed in her footsteps. Hell, most families in the projects were run by single mothers. *He ain't saying shit for real. It is easier with a two-parent home, I can't lie,* thought Shabria. *Ricoe's black ass is just so nasty in my bed! Imagine our ass walking around reeking of ass all around her kids all day. Mouth stay smelling* like butt *cracks and then some. Ricoe's nasty ass ain't got no problem getting out my bed like that, but I do.*

He can just get right up and start cooking like it ain't nothing wrong and shit. That's just plain nasty and trifling to me. Everybody that comes into my crib would be smelling what they did at night. Now, back in the day before having them kids that shit woulda been the bomb. But my ass is somebody's muva now and not some fast ass young thot! My babies ain't never been exposed to that nasty shit before. Ricoe ain't even they daddy for real. Shabria loved her man's dirty drawls and liked to sniff that shit for real. Just not when her babies was in the house. It just hit differently now as a single muva of two. Her ass can't be out here bringing random dick home in they house.

It just be's like that sometimes, thought Shabria. *I don't even walk around with my titties and ass out in front of my kids. I'll be damned if I let my man do that disrespectful shit if I'm not.* Shabria was just trying to set an example for her babies and ain't nothing wrong with that for real. After what went down with Neicy and her man, she was already feeling some type of way. Like her ass was coerced to going against her beliefs and shit. *That ain't right. I got to lower my standards so my new man won't cheat on me,* thought Shabria. *Love definitely can make yo' ass do some crazy fucked up thangs. To think, me and my homegirl done broke blood ties over some dick now. Twenty fucking years for a man who wasn't really all hers for real. Ricoe ain't even talking about putting no ring on it as it as. Wasn't nothing really official as far as I'm concerned. All my man can do is to promise me a wet ass every night and what good is that? We is still in the honeymoon phase and shit.* Like her mammy always said. "Shit don't happen until after the fucking ninety days is over." *Shit, they only been chopping it up for two months so what the fuck Ricoe?*

Ricoe as my man should have never put my ass in a position like that in this in the first place. His freaky ass could have rented a hotel room for all that. My mama, Tawanda done said a hundred times that she ain't watching Tyrik or Ti'aja. He stay thinking with the wrong head too much. I ain't forget how he blatantly pushed up on my sista girl right in my face. I love his chocolate ass to death bit I ain't no fucking fool now. Even my man heard about Neicy's thotting ass in these streets. He had to know of her because his ass was giving her too much attention and wasn't trying to be discreet about it either. Ain't no woman alive wanna see her bestie and her man cutting it up like that. That shit wasn't cute *or funny for real.* Shabria ain't like that foul shit at all. But her man did look real cute in that apron though. Shabria started smiling at his balls dangling in her tiny red apron. He looked mighty delicious and her mouth was watering to taste them. The kids was straight, so shouldn't her man be. Shabria ain't have no problem pleasing her man on her knees at all. She did and Ricoe called out her name over and over. She just had to remind him to whisper it and shit. "Ricoe, please baby! Not so loud. Moan using your inside voice." Her babies was at home, y'all.

"Baby, suck this shit. That's right, do Zaddy real nasty. Is yo' ass ready cause here it come. That's it! Swallow it all like a Queen!" he said as he tried to pull her hair off her head. Shabria liked that rough shit. Definitely don't knock it till you try it type

of fucking. Shabria did it to please her man and shit. But she still had a lot of shit on her mind though. Doing all that ain't really change the facts. As she wiped her face, she went back into her head.

That was only a part of they problems. Her and most single muva's still let they babies sleep in they bed.

***How can I do that shit now? My sheets is all sticky wet and shit. I ain't even got no incense to burn in here after sexting all night long. I don't even feel like going to the laundromat either. A bitch is tied and worn the fuck out for real,* thought Shabria. Tyrik and Ti'aja weren't exactly babies but they were *her babies*. Shabria had always kept them close at night and now that was about to change unexpectantly because of his ass. It was her unique way of bonding with them because they ain't going to be her babies forever. *Ain't nothing more precious as hearing yo' babies breathing right under your chest,* thought Shabria. Feeling they little heartbeats in sync with hers was the bomb for real. Now, out the blue, her ass was kicking them out her bed for Ricoe's black ass! As a muva, how that shit gonna look to them, right. She loved her man but what about her babies' habitable comfort zone? *Why does dating or being in a relationship got to be so fucking complicated*? she wondered. *With all those innocent kids getting gunned down and all them senseless murders in Baltimore. What else could a muva do to protect her own? Tragic times like that made yo' ass wanna keep yo' babies closer than close. A'int nobody promised tomorrow in they projects. Having a man is still good but at what costs,* she thought. Shabria had all kinds of crazy shit to consider for real. Ain't no guarantee in shit these days for real.**

Her ass was probably over thinking and shit as usual. But what if her whack ass baby daddy got released from Jessup and

shit. Tyrik can't rot in that jail cell forever. His ass fin to come home one fucking day. Ain't no telling when though is the real fucking question. Her and Ricoe's love thang was just too fucking toxic and complicated for her own blood and shit. It ain't matter that her and Ricoe was together because she vowed to always have her baby daddy's back, regardless.

Her ass wasn't about to see his ass homeless on no Baltimore City Street, for sure. That man's only crime was snitching to save his own ass at the end of the day. He did his time and is still fulfilling that bid because of it. She be dammed if her baby daddy is going to become the next victim in them streets. Fuck that because they kids was the bond that glued their asses together for life. His ass planted them pretty ass babies in her with that good ass hair, too. Ain't no way, she could lay down raw for a man all that time and not have his fucking back in his time of need. They could never be fucking enemies as far as she was concerned. All baby muva's and baby daddies fucked up from time to time. Ain't shit change but a dolla bill! They had history together. Blood, sweat and tears. ***Ricoe can't compare to that shit this fucking early,*** **thought Shabria.**

Shit, at the end of it all. Yo' ass is a baby muva or baby daddy for a reason for real. How is that shit gonna work when her ass is in a new toxic situationship though? Her baby daddy ain't gonna want another man in his bed and around his babies. Shabria couldn't stop thinking bout what her babies must have saw and smelled in that kitchen. It was time for her ass to speak the fuck up. She almost forgot where his head was at for about twenty freaking minutes. Shabria pulled his head up and told him to take a break for a minute. Just a minute though and then her man can go back to eating and shit.

"Bae, yo' ass know that people say shit in the heat of the moment, right? It is what it is! Is yo' ass really serious about moving the fuck in this crib is the question! You and I playing house and shit. I can't lie or front but the shit looks bomb from the outside. What about when shit hits the fan though, Bae? Is yo' ass gonna ride or die with me and my babies?"

"That wifey shit is glamorous as fuck, but is yo' ass really serious though? I ain't got time for games and shit. My babies is involved now, Ricoe! Wifey is and always will be that idol and role model for a single muva! But that was before I birthed two babies in the world, though. You feel me," said Shabria as she pushed the tray on the semen soaked sheets. Ricoe had the shit all figured out or at least his ass thought so.

"Why, the fuck not Shabria? We ain't getting no younger, a'ight! We is damn near pushing thirty. We is old as shit as it is. A playa gets tied of random ass sometimes. This had better not be about that clown ass baby daddy of yours. His ass is locked up, Shabria. How his simple ass gonna support you and his kids incarcerated, huh? Yo' ass barely got a pot to piss in as it is the way I see it! I pay for Lil' Tyrik's haircut at the barbershop on a regular. His ass already look up to me now. What other choice does he have, Shabria? I pay for Ti'aja's ballet lessons and shit like they is mines without question! I'm a good ass role model for them and yo' ass know that shit. I ain't out here standing on no fucking corner for that penny as shit. I ain't no gangbanger in the streets of Baltimore City, is I? I ain't never put my hands on no woman or went upside her head. Neicy ass deserved that shit so that don't count! My ass is a one in a zillion, believe that! My ass work and drive, Shabria. What else is there to consider? My black ass is drug and std free and shit! I even go to the store

to buy yo' fucking tampons and pads because I love yo' ass that much. I would stick it up in there if yo' ass asked me too! What's that old school song say, Bae? I'll even drink yo' bath water!" said Ricoe and he started tickling her silly.

Shabria heard him talking the talk, but it could also be bullshit too. It sounded good, but most things do in love.

He done already put it out there that he wants to fuck her best friend in her face, like what? His ass would do that shit at the first sign of trouble between them too. That was the only reason she let him stay the night in the first place. The only fucking reason for real. Ricoe continued all loud with his bullshit.

"As a matter of fact, my name around this bitch is going to be Black King, a'ight! Y'all stay calling me black ass all fucking day as it is. Why not put some respect on my shit while y'all at it? It only make sense to make my ass royalty!" preached Ricoe and his ass was dead serious too. *This shit is getting out of fucking hand now*, thought Shabria. Plus, she needed to check in wit her babies. They ass was awfully quiet out there as it was.

"Fool, yo' ass must have bumped yo' fucking head on my headboard last night! I ain't fin to call no man out here a king till his ass make me his official one and only Queen. My mama might uh been a fool but she damn sure ain't raise no fool, a'ight! I ain't one of those stupid ass girls that you use to fuck with in these here streets, Playa! I gots my head on straight like a mutherfucker, a'ight! I can't lie. Yo' ass do and can bring something to the table. Keep it mind that I been holding down the fort all this time. A single muva ain't no curse or the end of the world. Fuck that. It's 2021! I ain't got no problem being submissive and shit to my mans. It just has to be a fucking balance, Ricoe. I am that one fucking wifey that will move that dough if need to be! I want

to open my own salon and shit. Yo' ass still got me on that, right? Can't I be yo' woman and still have hopes and dreams. I might not can't do fucking hair but so the fuck what! If that's what I choose to do in my life, I am doing that shit regardless of my ability."

"I was planning on running my shit while these other hoes was my beauticians for real. I know I can't fucking braid hair or sow in a weave to save my life, Bae! The real question is what's going happen to our family if yo' ass got outta work and shit? That's what I be meaning when I say use the right head at the right time, Ricoe! The real question is where do that ass work at for real? Is yo' ass really a fucking chef and a poet though? I ain't never heard of you on no Amazon and I got Kindle Unlimited. What's yo' pen name and genre for real? I got to shake my head because they don't even go together for real. One minute yo' ass grew up in foster care and the next yo' ass was raised by yo' grandma, Ricoe! Which is it, huh? An orphaned boy or yo' ass got sisters and brothers. Make it make sense, for once. Is that homeless man, Tyrone yo' daddy or not?" laughed Shabria.

"I see yo' high yella ass got jokes and shit. Y'all thought that shit was hella funny last night! Yo' ass know that was yo' kid's baby daddy the whole fucking time, Bria! Yo' ass ain't holding shit down around here! Yo' ass ain't even got a flat screen and shit. Yo' crazy ass is still rocking with the DVD players in 2021! Yo' ass ain't even got hard plates and real silverware in this joint. Yo' cheap ass like using multi-colored plastic cuttery with those cheap ass foam plates and cups from the Dollar Store! Get the fuck out of here with that Miss. Independent jive, a'ight! Yo' ass needs to make it make sense for real. As only my girl, yo' ass don't need to know shit about how I move, a'ight. My personal

life ain't got shit to do with yo' ass! I ain't supposed to tell yo' ass how I move and why! Ain't nobody in Baltimore City know a Ricoe Jones and it's going to stay that way. They ass might know of me and that's about it! Yo' ass ain't no parole officer."

"Fuck all that!" and he walked over to kiss her. It was cool though because she was just about to kiss his ass too. They were kissing and all lovey dovey as usual until Ricoe wanted to crack slick again. But it was all good though, because ain't neither one of they asses was leaving.

"Since we is keeping it real and shit. Yo' girls ain't been keeping it 100 wit yo' ass. Cause yo' shit ain't cute at all, Sis. Out here looking like a fake ass SWV member and shit. Yo' ass could have at least sported the Total hairdo and shit. That short ass haircut was fire. I bought all they CD's back in the day. That hairdo yo' ass is sporting is in dire need of an upgrade, like seriously. Yo' ass out here looking like who dunnit and why? Yo' ass can't be my girl out here looking like that. Oh, and I know that homeless man is yo' daddy because yo' mama told me so last night!" laughed Ricoe as he hit her across the head with a pillow. *Did somebody say, pillow fight? Oh, it's on and popping* thought Shabria as she knocked him upside his face playfully.

They both was cracking up and enjoying the moment as usual. They were toxic as fuck together, but that was alright. It's something how two people can be bad and good for each other at the same time, right. They might as well had been since her relationship with Neicy was damn near done. Once a loyal blood chick do yo' ass dirty it's a wrap in her book. Throw the whole fucking twenty-year friendship in the trash. That was some straight-up foul shit to do to yo' sista girl over a man. Shabria put the whole blame on Neicy and not her own man. In a normal situation, how stupid is that? *Out of all the mens that hoe was sucking and fucking, Neicy had a nerve to thirst after hers, thought Shabria. That bitch was cruddy for that one. That bitch has a nerve to strut with high self-confidence.*

Her nasty ass was fine with sucking the main chick's juices of the man's dick on a regular. Who in they right mind does that nasty shit, thought Shabria? *It was trashy whores like Neicy that made it hard as fuck for women to keep they mans for real,* thought Shabria while laying on Ricoe's six-pack. He patted her head gently because he couldn't think of a better place to be right now. Shabria captured his heart almost instantly. It was love and lust at first sight for him.

"Sexy, yo' ass know you is my throat goat for life. That piece of paper shit don't mean crap for real. I see us jumping the broom down the line. My ass ain't never leaving you and my kids like that. I promise you that, my Queen. At nair one bitch out here got one over on yo' pretty ass. Remember that shit, a'ight. Lust is not the same as love. That soul tie shit ain't true at all. I ain't never fucked the same bitch twice. If I do, it's fin to be a problem then, a'ight!" said Ricoe but her ass wasn't paying him no attention when she should have. Real talk.

"Bae, yo' ass got friends though, right? I ain't insecure but what is yo' type? I mean what type of woman turns yo' ass on and shit?" asked Shabria while tracing her name on his chest with her fingers. Ricoe didn't know if he should answer that shit or not because he knew all women was insecure to some degree. Fuck it, her ass the one that asked.

"I like them phat wit thick hips and shit. Childless with a city girl attitude. A gangsta princess with hood mentalities and ghetto principles. Chocolate preferred. But my tongue is licking

a red-bone so what does that tell yo' ass, huh? I in due time, could see me and Neicy's ass patching our shit up down the line for real. If that's yo' girl than I should be friends with her ass, right?" said Ricoe with a big ass smile.

Sneaky ain't even the word to describe his ass for real. Friends with somebody his ass is highly attracted to and they feelings is mutual, too. **Shabria got up real quick and was ready to beat that ass over that fucked up shit.**

"Fuck no! No man should be friends with a bitch that they is attracted too! Especially, a freak like Neicy because yo' ass will cross the line if given the chance too. To me, Neicy sounds like yo' type as it is. It's too easy for a man to fall lustfully in love with what his ass can't have. That shit causes an unnecessary competition with the main chick. Especially if the friend is what he really desires! Her ass is everythang that I'm not, Stupid!" screamed Shabria. ***I can't even be honest with her ass for real,*** **thought Ricoe.**

"That shit ain't important right there. Just know if yo' ass ever cross me, yo' ass is dead to me, a'ight. If yo' ass start questioning me and shit, I is out! I won't take yo ass back at all. If I stay with yo' ass why is yo' ass worried about what I do for real and who I do it with? I can't have friends and shit now. If I gots to be on the end off yo' ball and chain, my black ass is out! If yo' ass can't trust me than." exclaimed his lying ass.

Shabria knew she was lighting a torch up his ass for that one. Forbidding her man would definitely make his ass do it more out of spite. Neicy's ass was just waiting in her shadows to fuck his face as it was. Ricoe was slick and knew how to lay the guilt trip on her ass thick.

"Bae, ain't no bitches or no niggas in my contacts or got my

number and yo' ass know that. Yo' ass is thee only one that I fucks with. Ricoe Jones moves by his damn self and always had. I ain't got a reason to fuck around with no other bitch! Be honored that I chose yo' ass over all them for real."

"Not any bitch can be crowned a wifey material, a'ight! Here I am thinking yo' ass is the one and yo' simple ass is starting to fuck it up over some dumb shit for real. I thought yo' ass was wifey material. Yo' ass stay fucking thangs up and shit. Like that homeless dude, my Queen. Why in the hell would I know of a homeless dude named Tyrone? I don't give a flying fuck what his ass said to y'all. I said I don't know him and that should have been the end of it for real. But yo' stupid ass kept running yo' mouth for nothing. I done told yo' ass the truth and you still don't believe nothing I say. I might as well fucking lie to yo' face then, right" hollered Ricoe. Shabria felt silly now. It was something how her man twisted her words up to turn around and make her ass look dumb for asking shit. Shabria figured that she had better not string his ass along. Besides, they was in love and invincible. *Fuck it*, she thought.

"Why not? We made it this far, right? I only lived with my baby daddy on and off. We wasn't ever committed like that for real. We can work this thang out, Black King! That's what you want my yella ass to call yo' ass right? I'm in, Bae!" said Shabria. It was all about living in the moment for the young lovers. Deal with tomorrow's shit when they got there. Everyday is a new day on the horizon.

Shabria decided right then and there to claim Black King as her prize. *Wasn't no other bitch fucking up they shit if she could help it. My ass done lucked the fuck up and snagged a real one. Ain't no throwing in no towel over a tiny lover's spat. Neicy's nasty ass sure*

wasn't getting wined and dined by my mans on gawd. That bitch had another thang coming if her ass tried that stupid ass shit again. Her ass slid by the first time with it. I be damn if her ass try it a second time though.

Now, that's what I wanna hear, **thought Ricoe. He did what any man would do in that situation. See what else that mouf do. He wanted to get his girl on a regular routine of servicing him whenever he pleased. It was Shabria's decision to accept the title of wifey. He ain't force her ass to do shit. Shabria was a grown ass woman at the end of the day so it is what it is. Ricoe lifted his apron and told her to crawl over to him and she obeyed like the obedient wifey. He guided her head down and grabbed the back of her hair softly this time. Shabria was doing it real good too. He was intentionally holding back because he wanted her to keep going and going. "Bae, don't stop. Ooh baby, do it to Zaddy just like that!" On that note, bad ass Tyrik burst through they door like a maniac. Little did Ricoe know but that was usually what her babies did. The last man was there was they daddy and they ass was in diapers. I guess it's a first time for everythang, then. "This Lil' nigga done lost his fucking mind, Shabria!" he said while forcibly pushing her head down on him. She still managed to jerk her head off him and pulled down the apron real fast. Shabria grabbed one sheet to cover her naked ass while using the end of it to wipe her mouth off.**

He gave her a look like yo' ass betta finish eating this dick up or else. Shabria worshipped the ground her man walked on for real. All she knew was that she was in love. That grown woman ass shit that these thots ain't know nothing about. If he asked her to, she would wipe his shitty ass for him if he couldn't for himself. That wasn't a problem for real. But your baby seeing a

penis in his muva's mouth was out the question. His ass had the nerve to expect her to finish with her baby in the room at that. After she got her and his ass respectfully together, she addressed her boy the best way she could.

Ricoe stood there pissed as fuck. It was quiet as shit all the sudden until he spoke. ***I ain't got to deal with this shit! Lil' man blocking my erection and shit.***

"Ma, why you on your knees like that in front of Mr. Ricoe? And his butt is all out. Eel, that look nasty!" said Tyrik obviously traumatized and horrified. That image would definitely be something that he'd never forget.

"Tyrik baby! Do you need something from mommy, Sweetie?" asked Shabria delicately. That was probably the wrong words to say at that time. Ricoe's nasty self was starting to stand at attention again. ***His nasty ass get hard over any old thang. But in front of my child is just creepy as fuck,*** **thought Shabria. Tyrik was looking at her man and his future stepdaddy in disgust. He was eight and not slow at all. Tyrik's smart behind formed his own theory of the situation before him. Tyrik almost dropped the jar of applesauce out his hands. "I don't but I think Mr. Ricoe does, Mommy," said little Tyrik.**

"Is it what he needs or I need Shabria? Lil' man ain't knock on the door or nothing for real. Tyrik yo' lil' ass is fucking eight and yo' fat ass can't open a fucking little ass jar of applesauce now. Shabria, is yo' ass going to leave me hanging wit blue balls as yo' man? Wifey, at this point once again, choose wisely!" Ricoe hollered.

Again, this was why she didn't like to bring her mens home. Her babies lived there for crying out loud. Her little family had a good thing going at home. She ain't never have to lock any door

but the front door in her apartment. Now, this shit first thing in the morning. Her kids were still acting as kids up until this point. Shit, they probably is the only kids in the projects that still played with fucking toys.

That was the way Shabria liked it. Keep them innocent, angelic and free from the evil nastiness of the world. *At least for now. Can't they be babies in peace*? Shabria prayed.

Now, my baby, Tyrik is forever traumatized by what he just seent, thought Shabria. *How in the hell can a single muva erase that shit? It's too fucking early to be explaining why I like to suck dick or about eating some pussy to a little eight-year-old. Just how,* she thought to herself. *It just should have never fucking happened. If I wasn't worrying about that nasty ass Neicy taking my man from me. This trifling shit would have never happened for real. I just can't with this shit. I feel like Ricoe ass is putting too much pressure on me. I love his black ass to the moon and back. But I can't be jumping through hoops and shit. What he* expect *me to do honestly*? thought Shabria.

"Ma, I just need help opening the applesauce jar. Ti'aja can't open it either, Ma. Somebody put it on too tight. It's not loose like it usually is," cried Tyrik. A lot of that crying was out of fear because he ain't understand what was really going on. Ricoe was ready to flip the fuck out and he did. He was tied of letting shit slide. This is the reason he ain't fuck with them single muvas like that. *Ain't this some shit, lil' nigga is already cock blocking. If I went home with phat ass Neicy I would not have had this fucking problem,* thought Ricoe. *Fuck that, this shit needs to be nipped in the bud. Shit, that's my mutherfucking motto in life. Her yella ass ain't acting like a wifey material. Whether she lived with a man like me or not, Shabria ass is going to learn today. If her ass don't know what time it is, she about to clock the fuck in for real. Tyrik whiny ass is on my time!*

"Wifey, I just fed his lil' fat, greedy ass! This is why yo' ass needs a man like me around. He ain't supposed to be whining and crying like no lil' bitch in front of a man."

"Tyrik, yo' ass is going to open that shit yo' self today. This barging in yo' parent's room like that is stopping now. Tyrik, when an adult has, they door closed, yo' ass supposed to knock first!" yelled Ricoe. Shabria instantly went into her motherly defense mode quick.

"In Tyrik's defense, how was he supposed to know yo' ass was still in here, Ricoe? He is only eight. This is why we need to have a talk first about you moving in here for real. I wanted to tell them about the new living arrangements first! I never intended for either " yelled Shabria.

"Fuck all that shit, Wifey! Sounds like yo' ass need permission to be the fucking adult in this bitch. I don't need his fucking approval. I'm a grown ass man with needs. His lil' snotty ass needs to stay in a child's place straight up. We is setting rules and boundaries in this bitch if yo' ass wants me to stay here or not. It's a whole lot of fucking places I can lay my head. Tyrik ass ain't starving! His ass needs to go the fuck on with that shit. Ain't no catering and pampering going to this lil' nigga over me no more! Yo' ass about to get him an ass whipping out chere in these streets," yelled Ricoe. Shabria was getting sick of his conceited ass.

"Tyrik, can you please wait for mommy in the kitchen? Me and Mr. Ricoe needs to talk, a'ight. Turn the radio or tv on real loud, too. It's too quiet!" said Shabria. Tyrik left with his head down.

"This is fucking sad! Yo' dumb ass gotta ask permission to set fucking rules! His ass ain't no fucking innocent! His ass probably already watching porn and shit as it is. The streets is telling his ass what yo' ass ain't. Real talk. His lil' bad ass probably a sneaky lil' mutherfucker too. Like I said. Is I'm living the fuck here or not, Wifey?" yelled Ricoe.

A sickening feeling came over her out the blue. It was just like the altercation with Neicy. *It was hard for her to explain it for real. I hate this shit when I'm arguing with my man. I feel like I'm losing his ass to Neicy every fucking time. It's like I can breathe on gawd. I must be severely lovesick and intoxicated over this man because it feel like I be dying inside and shit,* thought Shabria.

"Black King, please give me time. I need to have that man of the house convo wit my kids, a'ight. This can work. I know it can. I just hate to feel like I have to compete and shit. I saw the way yo' ass looked at Neicy and it scares me sometimes, a'ight! I know we is together like that and shit!" cried Shabria.

"Can I take a shower or do I need permission from yo' son? I got eyes so yes, I can look where the fuck I want too! If yo' ass gonna start whining and nagging and shit, I'm out. I ain't used to this shit for real. I'm going out after I wash my ass, a'ight. I need some fucking air. Yo' ass is starting to smother a brutha by emotionally controlling my ass!" said Ricoe as he headed to the shower. He did grab her bath towel to cover all the way before going out in the hall. If only his ass had used common sense and decency like that before. *His ass walking around my crib like his shit ain't stinking too,* thought Shabria. She ain't know what to do for real. Chase after his ass or tend to her babies. Her ass was in need of a shower or bathe too. Definitely a gargle and a toothbrush was overdue. Ricoe was in the shower singing and shit. *I wonder why his ass is in such a good mood all of the sudden. His nasty ass probably in there using my toothbrush and washcloth too. I hate it here. Why did have too fall head over heels in luv with his black ass so fast,* thought Shabria.

Shabria just sat on the bed with her head in the palms of her hand. Her mind was racing with thoughts of Neicy sucking her man off. She wondered if they had been fucking around behind her back this whole fucking time. Her intuition was definitely telling her ass that something was up and stuck. No sooner than she thought it, she saw and heard his phone vibrating on her dresser.

Should I answer that shit or not? I know it's a bitch disrespecting me while his ass in my fucking house! I got a right to sneak and unlick his shit for real. I is out here tossing that nigga's salad and then some. His black ass is staying in my bed. Why shouldn't I go through his fucking phone? I damn sure got a right to, thought Shabria sadly. She walked over confidently expecting to bust her man. Catch that ass cheating with proof. As soon as she picked it up, she had second thoughts. *What if he catches me, then what? I could lose him to her indefinitely* if *I'm wrong.* Shabria was thinking while unlocking her man's phone. What she read causes her already broken heart to skip a beat or two. She damned near flatlined when she read that shit. Ricoe was sick and funny as fuck.

Wifey, really! Yo' ass got to do better, the fuck. How is we going to make it if yo' ass don't even trust me. I know this is childish as fuck. Sending yo' ghetto ass a text to make yo' silly ass look stupid. As soon as it vibrated, yo' ass assumed that a bitch was texting yo' man. I done told yo' ass that I am not for the streets no more. Pick yo' pretty face up and join yo' soon to be husband in this shower, a'ight! I love yo' toxic ass with all my heart. Believe that shit!

Shabria did that shit real fast. Ricoe was too funny. He stayed

cracking her silly ass up. ***I guess I can let my guard down then. My man don't want no nasty ass Neicy.***

It's all about me and mines. I ain't even got to worry about no other bitch at the end of the day. I just got to lighten up and go against my intuition, I think.

Fresh out the shower with her smell good on and shit. Today was going to be a good day because she could feel it. They talked in the shower and set some ground rules and they was good. Her man ***was moving the fuck in*** **and that was going to solve all her problems or so she thought.**

Within minutes, Ricoe was dressed, with keys in hand and jacket on. All she could do was to smile to keep from crying. Shabria ain't want to let her man out her sight for real. ***Maybe my King is going to his crib to pack his shit. He gots to do a change of address for his mail soon anyway. Maybe he is going to MVA to change his address on his license. I just lovee me some him and by his actions he's still very much in love with my ass, too. I hope I ain't mess things up with him again.***

"A'ight, catch yo' ass later. I'm out," said Ricoe as he was leaving their bedroom. He ain't said nothing else though.

No kiss goodbye or nothing. ***What the fuck is up with that? Oh lordt, here we go again with this fool. It's like we is good one minute and the next his ass is shitty and sneaky with me. I don't like that shit and I done told his ass a thousand times. Is his ass playing games? What the fuck Ricoe, Remy or whatever yo' government name is?***

"Black King, I don't want to be clingy or petty for real. But where is yo' ass going so quick? We just got out of the fucking shower and shit!" said Shabria. That crummy feeling was back. Her anxiety was back and kicking her ass again. Ricoe look dead at her and continued to leave.

"How yo' ass going ask yo' own questions and answer that shit too? Yo' crazy ass is too fucking funny."

"I spent one fucking night and yo' ass is already questioning where I go," he laughed and shut the door behind him. Ricoe ain't even give her the chance to respond. He just dipped, dipped.

Shabria went straight to her cellphone. *I needs a stat 911 sista girl chat, like now. The fuck! It' ain't gonna be that nasty ass Neicy! So, it gots to be my girl, Trina then.* Shabria dialed her only friend in the world. Trina came in ten minutes like a real bestie would. Even though they ain't talk like that because of her new man and shit. Trina always had her back and shit. Trina was the true ride or die bitch. Ain't too many bitches going vouch for yo' ass when yo' ass is clearly treating them greasy as shit.

Shabria heard her out there in the living room talking to Ti'aja and Tyrik. They was laughing and shit so that was a fucking good sign. Bria needed that time to get her shit together for real. Fix her face and shit. Definitely wipes her tears and all that black mascara running down her face. Too late, her ass came barging through her bedroom door. At least her face was straight. It was time to put up a front and shit.

"Oh, hey Sis! I been trying to call yo' ass but my phone been acting stupid as shit. I done paid all this fucking money for it and it still ain't shit. Sis, yo' ass look good. All glowing and shit. Is yo' ass in luv too?" lied Shabria.

"I see yo' yella ass is on some funny shit already, huh. It's too fucking early in the day for that shit for real. I ain't never been the bitch that kissed and tellt, have I? How long we been sistas, Shabria? My point exactly! I don't put my personal business out in the fucking street, especially now. Yo' ass should know that. That's yo' crazy ass thang. *I moves by my damn self, a'ight.* So, what is this shit about really?"

"I ain't come all the way over here to rat on Neicy's ass either. As for yo' man, that's y'alls problem. You and fucking Ricoe's toxic shit. I don't want to be in no parts of that shit, a'ight. If it's anything else, I'm down Sis. My black ass is loyal to everybody and that's the way I is. Now, continue from this part. Please and thank-you," said Trina seriously.

I don't know why her black is here then. If a bitch can't spill the tea what I need her to. Her ass definitely know some dirt. Them quiet, sneaky ass ones always do. If the fucking streets is talking, trust and believe this bitch knows all about it. As a sistahood, we need to stick the fuck together. But this hoe on some other funny shit, I see. Loyal, my ass. Whatever happened to the damn sistacode? If yo' ass see or hear something, say something. What the fuck? I damn sure would have did the same for her trifling ass!

Shabria tried to play it off the best way she could. That was exactly the reason she decided to call Trina and the only one. It is what it is because they really ain't mess with each other like that no more. Was it because she got a new man or not?

"I can't miss my besties. Even Neicy for real. I don't got a beef with her. For what, Trina?" lied Shabria.

That was the thing. Until she knew who's side Trina was on, Shabria had to play it cool. If her girl was on her side and loyal, her ass would have been done spilt the tea on Neicy. Trina could even have come over to benefit that nasty Neicy. Shabria knew how the ladies got down. That's why she only fucked with two of them hoes and even they couldn't be trusted here lately. Shabria knew one damn thing. Her ass wasn't stupid enough to spill the tea on her own problems and shit. So, Trina can run her mouth to Neicy.

Ain't no way I am helping the bitch take my man away. Uh-uh, Sis! Not fucking today. I know betta than that. Trina's sneaky ass ain't slick.

"Just checking because a bitch ain't got time for dumb shit, a'ight. And yes, I do got a man. And it is none ya, so don't ask. We is good and it is what it is. We is both winning! I was about to chop it up wit him when I got yo' 911 emergency text. So, what gives, Bria? What is this shit all about for real? Me and my man can't go out often as it is. What's up?" said Trina without making any eye contact. But her crazy ass was always weird like that.

"Nothing. I done told yo' ass that my phone is a piece of shit. Fill me in on what's going on with Facebook and shit. What I miss?" asked Shabria who was still obviously pissed the fuck off. Trina was acting all stupid and looking down at the floor and shit. *What's up wit this slow ass bitch for real? I know her weird ass ain't fucking wit my mans too. What the fuck am I saying? Trina James ain't even my man's type and shit. Ain't no way he creeping wit this bitch too!*

"About that. I unfriended yo' ass and blocked yo' ass for real. I don't what's up with Neicy other than she is fucking somebody's man I suppose. Don't worry red-bone. We is still cool as shit or I wouldn't have came the fuck over here. It is personal Love. So, I don't know what I can tell yo' ass." Trina was being a little to comfortable with hinting around and shit. Shabria was about ready to cuss her no good ass out.

"I see yo' man gave the kids two envelopes with two-hundred a piece in it though. Lil Tyrik showed me. Lil Ti'aja grown ass already done said what she going to do with hers and shit. They got a real good stepdaddy on their hands."

" I hope I get a good baby daddy like Ricoe one day. Anyways

though Boo, my ass is going out shopping too," said Trina with a big Kool-Aid smile on her face. *That's a first,* thought Shabria.

"Oh, I totally understand the social media thing. I wouldn't been on there like that either, even if my phone was fixed Girl. But it was good to finally meet up with yo' ass, girl. How is Neicy though?" Shabria found it easy to pretend to care about her grimy ass. Trina started smiling and twirling her hair in imaginary wind.

"Oh, I don't know. The streets is saying she got her a new man. But I ain't checking for the bitch anyways because I gots my own when he has the time to get away. I'm still cool with her and you too. We are three grown ass women, Shabria. What we look like beefing over some man, right. I guess we is all going to be booed up with our mans this winter. Well, look he is waiting on my pretty chocolate ass to come through for real. We gots to get together more like this. Kick it like we use to and shit. Our whole lives we shared everythang. It feels good as shit to have something or someone of my own. I lovee my new friend and shit. Bria, he is a dream come true too. Well smooches. He is texting Baby, where it at? If yo' ass know what I mean," and they kissed each other on the cheek. Shabria wriggled her nose because Trina's shirt smelled familiar as shit. *What is that scent cause I damn sure smelt that shit before? Is I'm losing my mind cause it damn sure feel like it. Everyman can wear the same fucking cologne. Trina's ass just needs to go!*

"Ok, Girl! I hear that shit. I am really happy for yo' ass and Neicy too. We finally got something real. Us project chicks need love too. Yass, we got to chop it up and kick it like the good old days for real. Nice seeing yo' pretty self and shit. Take care," lied Shabria. Just like that another bestie was out of her life. All over

a man. Hopefully not hers, though.

After she got herself together, she went to check on her babies. It was a good time to talk wit her kids about they new living conditions. Shabria didn't want no more surprises like the last night. Her kids was getting a new live-in stepdaddy. There was bound to be some attitudes and adjustments.

They was in the living room like most kids at that age. Their room was too small so where else is they going for real. No porch, balcony or backyard or shit. One small ass bathroom. Tiny ass kitchen and living room. It was about to be crowed as shit in they crib. Tyrik was playing Roblox on his phone while Ti'aja was making TikTok videos.

"Hey, y'all listen up. Turn yo' phones off. Power it down, Ti'aja before I snatch it. Look guys! I know there's been some new changes around here. A new man in particular. Mommy's new friend. Well technically not new. Y'all met him before and even hung out with him a few times," said Shabria slowly. There was no right words to say the wrong things. The new man was taking they daddy's place and to make matters worse Ricoe had moved in already too.

"He a'ight though Ma. He gave us these envelopes and we can't wait to see what's in it. We was waiting on you Ma because you said don't taking money from strangers, right. You can't even see through the envelope for real," said Tyrik and he started shaking the envelope for coins. Shabria thought that shit was weird because Trina's sneaky ass acted like she knew what was in it already. *Let my silly ass stop. My man is probably home packing his shit for my crazy ass as I speak. I don't know what is wrong with my ass. I gots me a real good man this time.*

"It is more than him giving you a couple of dollas', Son. Ti, baby how you feel about Mr. Ricoe? I know he ain't yo' daddy but he loves y'all like his own," said Shabria as she pretended to brush her daughter's long pretty hair. Ti'aja just gave her that look.

"He done moved in our place already so what difference does that make? Ma, where is daddy going to live then? You been saying our daddy in the Army for years. We think daddy is just in jail, Ma. Don't you think that a convo about our daddy should come first?" said six-year old, smart ass Ti'aja. *I is catching a charge for this one today, no doubt.*

"Ma, don't get mad at Lil' Ti. But that's true and I ain't tell her nothing. This is our daddy's house and we never conversate about him. Why is that? Mr. Ricoe is a'ight but living here though with us. I ain't no Einstein or nothing but I think that would be dumb on your part, Ma! All of us cramped up like roaches in a small box though. He's already taking over as it is, Ma. Do we even have a choice in the matter for real," said Tyrik. Shabria was not ready for that conversation at all. If it was up to her, she would have never brought her baby daddy up. She was in love and in a new relationship. Shabria didn't want to go there after all she had gone through with his trifling ass. Ricoe was right and they ass was not no fucking babies no more. Look how grown-up they was talking and shit.

"Here's the thing, Y'all. Mommy is grown and yo' daddy is not here. I don't know if he's coming back or not. Ti, yo' lil' self is right. Yo' daddy is in jail for some dumb shit. I can't tell you what I don't even know, a'ight. Why do y'all insist on punishing mommy for his mistakes. I get lonely too you know. I can't spend the rest of my life waiting on him, guys. Y'all will be teenagers before you know it."

It's going to come a time when y'all going to want to go out and do yo' own thang yourselves. I don't want to become a lonely old woman. Besides, as the adult in charge." Shabria stood up because she felt like she was losing control at the family meeting. It made her think of what her man done told her about rules and shit in her household. *I'll be damned if I let they snotty lil' noses dictate to me. I did the best I could for these brats as it is. They should be happy that they mama is not all sad and miserable.*

"I don't need y'alls permission to do anything for real. Mr. Ricoe is a part of our family whether y'all like it or not. I ain't going to be tiptoeing around my own apartment no more. Especially, when I'm the only one paying bills around here, you two. Mr. Ricoe is a real good man. Just give him a fair chance and y'all will see for yo 'selves. Trust yo' mommy on this one. Haven't I always had your back. Just because there's a new man in my life, I am still the mommy! I know what I'm doing and that's that!" yelled Shabria with her hands on her narrow hips. That was the one other thing that Neicy had over her. Out the three of them, old nasty ass was blessed with the womanly body. Her phat ass filled out at a lil' old thirteen-years of age. Neicy had melon boobs, thick hips and curvy thighs. Not to mention that real phat ass that her man couldn't stop staring at.

"He still not my daddy. You is right. This is your place, Ma to do as you please. Me and Tyrik just live here," said smarty pants. Shabria was ready to smack her little girl in her sassy mouth. Luckily, Tyrik was there to grab her hand away.

"Ma, Ti didn't mean any of that. If that's what makes you happy," said Tyrik out of fear. "I prefer to have my daddy here, but he ain't. I can't get mad at you because of that. If that's what you really want to do. He ain't going to be bossing us around

though. If that's the case, let us live with Granny then. Granny, got a Firestick and fast Wi-Fi on a flat screen, anyway. Just if our daddy ever comes home, we might decide to live with him. Giving he is our real dad and all," said Tyrik all serious like.

"I can do that, y'all. That's not a problem. Just respect him and our privacy, a'ight. Y'all got to start knocking on mommy and daddy's bedroom door now. It's about time for y'all to start sleeping in yo' own beds too, a'ight," said Shabria confidently.

"Can you at least tell the new stepdaddy to buy us some beds first. We been done outgrew our toddler beds years ago, Ma. I know the state is giving you some type of check since our daddy is in jail. A lot of my friend's mothers is on Social Services and they is doing real good. Their fridge stay full with them food stamps," said Miss. Grownie. Shabria was ready to be that ass but decided not to. Instead, she wanted to give her kids a lesson about life instead.

"Listen hear, Ti'aja Arielle Wilson and listen real good! There ain't nothing wrong with being independent and doing for you and yours. I am not the type of mama to take no government handouts. I surely don't knock the mother's that do. Social Services is not a career choice, young lady. Who wants to be trapped in the projects for the rest of their lives doing nothing. If you get a job and try to do better, they cut you off. You make too much; Section 8 will raise your rent up to more than you can afford. You got to live where they tell you and shit. Your babies is failing in these ghetto, inner-city schools. I want more than that for y'all. Go out and get a job and see the real world. Life has so much more to offer, y'all."

"But Ma, you are only looking at one side of it though. It's not that bad if that's what they choose to do. Some people is just

content with a familiar environment. They could be scared of change and what lies ahead. All you see is the negative side of poverty. Some of the low-income families is doing really good for themselves. The parents and they kids go off to become doctors, nurses, lawyers and rappers though."

"A'ight, I see your point Tyrik. Just know that this was my decision and I still stand by it no matter what. So, let's just leave that one alone for now. All I was saying is that y'all need to be sleeping in your own beds from now on, Tyrik and Ti'aja."

"Ma, have you seent our baby beds, lately? We had them since me and Tyrik was two. We ain't want to bunched up and all crooked in that raggedy bed of ours, feel me. That was one of the main reasons that me and Tyrik slept in your bed, Mommy," said Lil' Miss. Six going on sixteen.

The only other complaint her kids had was they stepdaddy being nasty looking in her apron. They ain't want to see all that mess. They was fine just eating cereal and milk for they breakfast. Nobody asked stinky to go all out for them and cook they breakfast. They wasn't used to that for real. *At least we is all laughing and joking about the new stepdaddy, so it was all good,* thought Shabria. *But where the fuck is my mans at? His ass ain't call, text or nothing all day.*

Shabria was tied of checking her phone every second to see if his ass texted back or not. After a while, she started texting threats to his sneaky black ass. *If he ain't answering his girl's text that ass is definitely in another bitch's face.* All her calls eventually started routing straight to fucking voicemail. That was after she left over a hundred thirsty ass voice messages. *Shit, I can't do this. What can us ladies do when our mans fuck up, right? Spend his fucking money if the hoe got any. I still got that nigga's checkbook*

and credit card in my purse and what. These are the trying times when I wish I had my two besties rocking with me and shit. Damn. I miss they ass. Why men got to always fuck up the sista code and shit. A bitch need her girls. The ride or dies right about now on gawd. But I guess Riff and Raff lil' asses will have to play they part. Ain't nobody else for real.

"Kids, lets go! Get y'alls coat and put on yo' shoes cause Mr. Ricoe wants his family to go a shopping today, a'ight! Now!" Shabria felt like she had to do something other than lose her fucking mind over her boyfriend like that. *I don't know where his black ass is or where he lay his head at for real. It's only one thing that I can do. Go find his ass and make him come home.* Shabria had it all figured out too.

"We is going to Mondawmin Mall this time. I hear that got some good deals over west for real," hollered Shabria. Her ass ain't know a thing. She was going over West Baltimore to try to spot out her man. *As big as West Side is, how is I'm going to find him for real. That nigga obviously don't want to be caught or he would have texted my ass back by now. I tell ya. These men ain't no fucking good!*

I know somethings got to give for real. Maybe, I can spot one of his cars or at least something. Ricoe can't just up and disappear like that. Somebody done seen something now. They fucking had to! If a bitch calls my man, my sexy voice is on his answering message. Hell, both our faces is on his screensaver and lock screen for real. The streets had to know who I am and shit. Plus, we been kicking it all over East Baltimore in broad daylight for a minute now, shidd. Everybody in the fucking projects know we is together like that.

"Ma, why got to go all the way to the inner city when we got a Dollar Store right by the apartment. We is closer to Eastpoint

Mall and they probably got the same thing. That's a long ride," said Tyrik while huffing and puffing.

It was definitely the truth. That mess ain't make no sense at all. The kids was wondering why they mama was geeking like that. Driving on the west side just because.

"I is the driver and y'all got to go where I tell y'all to go. I'm in charge around here and y'all better not forget it." Shabria had to laugh to keep from crying because she knew that was a stupid move. Especially, when bringing her kids along due to her bubbling insecurities. The kids should never be involved in grown folks mess like that. It was just dumb and reckless on her part. Ti'aja's grown tail had her eyes submerged in the envelope like what the fuck. That lil' girl's facial expression was priceless.

"We need to go to the Dollar Store for sure with this paper! Tyrik, we ain't going to no Price Busters today. Our beds done gone out the window for today. I got all pumped for nothing, again. Our supposedly rich stepdaddy done gave us twenty-dollars. He could have gave us this little bit of money in our hand for real. Why he had to be extra by putting it all in a sealed envelope? And it was wrapped like we was getting a real surprise, too. I guess the surprise is really on us then!" said lil' grownie. Ti'aja scrunched her lil' face like oh really now. It didn't take long for Tyrik to feel some type of way either. It ain't make no sense to drive anywhere with that.

They could save a long trip by just walking up to they corner store for real. Shabria felt real dumb because she was expecting much more this time. *His ass got jokes, I see.*

Trina's ass done said it was two-hundred fucking dollas'! Then where it at then? How she know what my man did first of all. That bitch better not be wallet watching on my fucking man. Fuck her, I got

bigger problems than that! My mans claim to *have two fucking jobs, so where the money at then?*

"Well, I still got to go out Mondawmin to pay on my layaway anyway, y'all! We is going and that's that. They got discount stores there too!" Shabria was pissing her own self off because she knew she wasn't making no sense now. Tyrik had to get on her in a respectable way of course. He didn't want to blow up her spot by making her look silly. But hey, it had to be said or they would have been driving for nothing for real.

"I don't mean no harm, Ma. But I don't think stores do no layaways like that no more. Ma, it is 2021. Who still does that for real? Especially in the city nowadays. I don't even feel like going for real. Me and Ti heard y'all all last night and into the morning. I'm tied and sleepy for real." Tyrik was right on point wit that one.

Shabria was so embarrassed that her face turnt blood red. *Shit, they ass done heard us fucking. See, that's why I ain't want to do that shit in they house with my kids in the next room. It's not like they infants like my man done said. I can't give they asses no Similac bottle wit the baby cereal in it no more. They ass was too big to be sleeping through the night and shit! I don't know where my head be at sometimes. Let me stop, cause I do know where exactly where it supposed to be every night. Right between my King's legs faithfully. That's how it posed to be as wifey!*

"Ma, you is better than me cause my barbies don't play that. All them Barbie Girls made they Ken's buy them a dream house and a car first," and Ti'aja shook her lil' head.

"You have to do what you have to do sometimes, Ma. If you know we need something speak up. If Mr. Ricoe ain't helping all of us than why is he here then? The twin beds is like a hundred dollars in the circulator paper this week. It's bad enough that our rooms is side by side as it is, Ma! I already done seen and heard that mess at school, too. Y'all adults is just so nasty! Can't we get a bigger place or naw?" said Ti'aja.

"You know what I can't with y'all today! I guess it is time to talk to y'all about the birds and the bees then. I swear y'all babies grow up so fucking fast! Jeez, here my stupid tail think y'all mind is pure and unvulgar," laughed Shabria with them.

"Ain't no birds out there. Them lil grown ass girls is doing the butterfly for real letting every lil' tick hit, but not me. Ma. They doing it for Now Later and Hot Chips. You do you, Ma but I would still ask him though," said Ti'aja all serious and shit. Tyrik hunched his shoulders like oh well then.

"She is right though Ma. Ain't enough room in here for no fourth person now. Y'all done already broke y'all headboard off last night. Ain't nobody want to be hearing that all day and night. Besides, me and Ti'aja is too big to be sharing rooms now. Ma, I'm is eight, for real!" Tyrik did speak the truth loud and clear. Shabria knew her kids was right. *But how would her man feel about that?*

"Ok, I get it. When he get in, I'll ask him about it and see what he says. So, y'all want to hangout or something today. We can go to the five-dolla matinee on Belair Road, if y'all want. Skating or do something because it's still early out. We ain't got to stay cooped up in here all day. I do have y'all stepdaddy's credit card and check book on me!" said Shabria with a smile.

Tyrik looked in his envelope and made a face. "Not me, I see he is doing tick for tack wit me. I only got ten-dollas over that applesauce jar earlier and that's crazy. I see how it is for real. I ain't even going to worry about it for real. Let L' Cheapo keep his coins, I'm good! I see that I'm already going to have to change my ways right quick, Ma. I can't be whining and crying around no street thug like that, Mr. Ricoe. He fin to roast me in my own crib over that. Mr. Ricoe plays hard-ball and I can roll with that. It's been time for me to man up around here, Ma. Our daddy ain't here, so Mr. Ricoe will have to do right now. I mean at least for the time being. I pray to God that our real daddy gets out one day for real. I mean I ain't got nothing against your boyfriend for real. Ma, you like what you like. But at least make it work for all of us. Me and Ti should always come first because we is your kids. Mr. Ricoe can do better with it. You shouldn't even have to ask for a bigger place or new beds for us. If he living here, he should already known that."

"He said he work downtown at the post office at night and do security at the bank in the morning. At least you got a working one this time, Ma," smiled Tyrik.

"It seems that Mr. Ricoe works all over the city for real. I done heard it all. I am definitely going to holla at him when he gets in here! He is apparently a chef, a poet, a postal worker and a security guard now. But like you said. He do work and that's exactly what our family needs right now because the struggle is real. Tyrik you is right about that jar of applesauce though. I know he ain't yo' daddy. Believe me when I say that he can never take yo' daddy's place. He was just looking out for you man to young man that's all. It's just that adults have to do what is right for them is all I'm saying."

"Y'all daddy done made a grown-up decision years ago and got to pay the price for it. I wasn't intentionally keeping y'all from going to see him. But prison though, Tyrik. I ain't think y'all would have wanted to see yo' daddy in handcuffs in no jail cell like that. But that is something that I am willing to do. I want him to meet Mr. Ricoe one day for real. I don't feel right sneaking behind his back. There is a new man in our lives so they might as well get along for y'alls sake. It comes a time we need to act like mature adults. Y'all feel me?" Shabria was trying to convince herself of that bullshit because she knew it was not going to go like that at all. That was her baby daddy's crib right there. Ain't no doubt in her mind that he wouldn't want *his* place back when or if he got released. After doing a bid like that too. *Where else is he gonna go if released?*

I know one damn thing! It's due time for my king to pay the piper for real. We is having a real serious chat when he come strolling in here. It may not be what he want to hear, but oh well. Even in jail, my baby daddy has a lot to say about our shit for real. He is going to expect Ricoe to at least do right by us since he is fucking his baby muva and shit. I don't know when his ass is getting the fuck out and it makes no difference to me one way or the other. I don't even be talking to dude like that for real but I still respect him as my kid's father regardless of the situation between us. I got to give that man respect. Ricoe might not want to go, but I damn sure plan on!

"They wound up just kicking it at home and shit. Shabria had a couple of bootleg DVDs that they ain't see anyway. They stayed in and ordered carryout. Time went by real fast because before they knew it the streetlights flickered on. It was damn near eight a clock for real. Still no signs of her man in sight. *Maybe he is working or maybe he not.*

I just have to wait it out and see. Ain't nothing I can really do about it for real. I done got myself invested too fast in this dude. It ain't like I can turn back the hands of time now. I already done gave it up too soon as it is. His black ass has supposedly already moved in here according to him. I know my man got some bright ass real flags and shit. They is fanning right in my face and I know that I should be done for real. This love thang is too fucking complicated. I done let this man wear my heart on his sleeves now. What I'm a do now? Take it back and start over then. His ass already got me sucking and tossing his salad as it is. Next, he probably going to want my ass to do some freaky shit like pegging and golden showers next. He definitely is going to upgrading me from wifey to fucking Mrs. Ricoe Jones and shit for all that! I ain't got a problem with doing none of that shit if his ass is faithful and respect me as the main chick. That is my current situation. See how love can get yo' ass in all types of dilemmas!

At one am, his ass had the nerve to come in with flowers and shit. His ass smelling like weed and a few other things. He cut on her bedroom light because his drunk ass done tripped over the tv stand and shit. He was smiling as he handed her a wrinkled piece of paper and shit. Shabria snatched that shit right out of his ashy hands. Damned near breaking and crushing his fingers back.

"What the fuck is this shit for, Ricoe? Where yo' ass been all fucking day. I been calling and texting yo' ass all day. Is this how we do now, huh? I stay home while yo' ass play in the fucking streets still. When did the wifey role switch up to play the dummy face? Yo' ass ain't come in here with no packed bags or nothing! I gave yo' ass the benefit of the doubt and it backfired!" Shabria ain't see no suitcases or duffle bags. "What the fuck is the dried up, stanking roses going to do, Fool? It damn sure ain't no peace offering. You can stick that shit with its thorns right up your ass for real. Yo' ass done left my kids with thirty freaking dollas' between them, too! And it was nice outside," hollered Shabria.

Ricoe obviously was not in the right shape or form to argue

and shit. He done had one helluva day and that's real shit. He just wanted to get into her bed and sleep for real. He wasn't for her ass yelling and screaming over some dumb shit. *This is why I live the fuck alone. I come and go as I want to and ain't got to answer to no bitch!*

"Thirty-dollas and yo' silly ass is tripping. Yo' baby daddy ain't even got that to his name? Yo' ass know that orange jump-suit nigga is broke as shit. Before I be's a snitch, I'm at least going to make sure my girl and kids is straight. What the fuck, Shabria? I ain't have to do that shit if I ain't want too. I'm just they stepdaddy, a'ight. Take that funny shit up wit the baby daddy. I'm tied as shit and want to go the fuck asleep. Is that too much to ask for, Wifey. I gave them thirty dolla's because that's all they needed. Ain't no free handouts for nobody, Love. They want more they asses got to earn it just like the rest of us. Shit, at that age kids be having chores and shit, a'ight." Ricoe sat on the edge of the bed and started taking off his shoes and shit.

"Oh yeah, like you and yo' brothers and sisters did, huh. One minute yo' ass ain't got no family and growing up in foster care and shit. The next, yo' ass done got siblings and y'all was raised by yo' granny and shit. Which is it for real?" Shabria looked at the crumbled piece of paper. It appeared to be some whack ass poetry and shit. *Fuck a poem, you old lying, cheating dog! Go back to that bitches house that you came from.*

"I done wrote yo' dumb ass a poem and shit, silly. Can't yo' king switch it up and be romantic sometimes, damn?" I done got yo' ass roses and everything and yo' ass is still bitching and complaining. I don't get it because I came home like yo' ass demanded and shit," hollered Ricoe. Shabria stood in front of his intoxicated ass with her hands on her hips. Shabria was ready to chew his ass out over that bullshit.

"Negro, I want to know where yo' bags is, shit! Is yo' ass moving in or not? Don't have my ass out here looking like BoBo the Clown and shit. Yo' lying ass is just sneaky as fuck. I don't even know the basic shit about yo' ass, my King. I mean who the fuck is Ricoe Jones for real? Like where that ass work at and what's up with yo' family and shit like that, Ricoe? After she said it, Shabria realized that she ran her mouth a little too much.

"Is yo' ass fucking with me or my family, Shabria? So, it don't matter what I said! I'm a working brutha and that's all yo' ass needs to know. I ain't smell no dinner when I came home and shit, Wifey. Where yo' mans food at? Damn, I should never said that shit to yo' nasty ass because now, I'm going have lockjaw tonight and a broken neck. When yo' freaky ass sit on my face, I swear yo' ass be trying to break my neck. Especially, when you is mad at me for real. Just remember that if yo' ass do intentionally try to hurt me, you ain't getting shit out of me. We ain't even married yet. Sorry, my Queen but ain't no alimony check coming for that ass from me! Just kidding but yo' ass stay riding the wrong thangs, Sweetheart. When a man come home, the wifey is supposed to be riding his dick only. Ain't no man want to come home to no fucking nagging like that. If I can't find peace at home, where is I'm supposed to go, Wifey."

"My bags and shit ain't packed because my lease ain't up yet. If I got to pay the rent at my apartment every month than I might as well keep it, right. How many men out here can afford to do that? I'm paying my girl's place and mines. Just relax and stop keep blowing thangs out of proportion all the fucking time, a'ight! Is there anything else on yo' mind, my Queen before I crash?" he said calmly.

Now, that was the type of shit that made her blood boil right there. Ricoe was always flipping the script to make her look like the bad guy in every argument or fight. It was clear as day that his ass was in the wrong again with his sneaky ass. There was a lot of shit on her mind at the moment. The question was whether she should go there or not. *Fuck it cause it is what is. I still got questions about what my girl Trina done said earlier. Something about her kid's envelopes ain't make no sense to her. A part of me is saying don't rock the boat. The other part is saying to fucking sink that boat and throw away his lifejacket for real. Drown that ass for lying to her face like that. He got a whole Bae Watch beauty at home for all this.*

"Well, there is something My king before I ride yo' ass like a cowgirl! Trina came by after yo' ass left and." Shabria got cut off real quick. *Oh, that's real fucking rude!*

Ol' Ricoe got real defensive and loud. His whole composure had done changed. His ass done turned real evil and mad as fuck. Why, was the question? Shabria started wondering why his ass was giving all that attitude over it. Trina is still her best friend and shit. Her and Trina went back to twenty years of friendship together. Besides, his name wasn't even on her lease yet.

"Wayment. What is *her* ass doing over here when I ain't home? I keep telling yo' ass to watch yo' girlfriends and shit. Yo' dumb ass is still not hearing me though. I don't ever want to see that bitch in *this crib.* I ain't got to be on yo' lease to enforce that shit either. If I'm going be staying here and paying bills and shit, I call the fucking shots, too. I got a problem with both of them two whores for real, a'ight. Just leave it alone and concentrate on me and you! Now, tell me something good, my Queen because I am shutting this fuckery down stat, a'ight." Just like

that he ended the conversation that his dumb ass started. Shabria wasn't too worried about it right now because she had bigger fish to fry.

"A'ight. A'ight. Please calm the fuck down. We ordered carry-out and there is pizza and wings in the fridge. I would have heated it up if yo' ass if you had at least text me back. All you had to say was yo' ass is on the way. You don't want them in our crib, fine then. It ain't that serious Ricoe! I will tell yo' ass what is serious though. It's simple. If we all going to be cramped up like this, we is going to need a house or something. Tyrik and Ti'aja is going to need they own room and shit. We all need our own space and the one tiny bathroom we got here has got to go." Ricoe gave her the I don't know about all that look and Shabria was furious.

"How is the four of us going to share one fucking toilet, huh? My little closet ain't that big as it is! Other than that, we is always going to be good no matter what, my King. I want us to make it as a couple. It ain't all that easy, but nothing worth saving ever is!" said Shabria while sitting on his lap. She started pulling off his shirt and kissing on his neck. He gently pushed her away and was trying to play that shit off. Shabria wasn't letting that shit slide too.

"Bae, what's wrong tonight? This is my wifely duty to please my man right. I'm already over Neicy and Trina's ass. "Yo' ass don't want them here, that's already done. Look Bae, communication is key to us surviving now. I should be asking you about what's on yo' mind tonight? Yo' ass is too distracted and snappy. I'm about to call yo' ass a Ninja Turtle if yo' ass keep changing up and shit. Tell me what's going on in that head of yours. Come on and talk to me now." Said Shabria as sweetly as she could. She

ain't like her man turning down sex and shit, but what else could she do? She couldn't just force herself on him if he wasn't in the mood for some reason. Shabria was obviously shocked and definitely hurt over it. Shabria started to think that he was probably just tied of sexing her and shit. It was just way too early in they relationship for that foolishness.

"It ain't you. I'm just tied and want to sleep right now. If I fuck yo' ass, I got to take a shower first and shit. I just came in for real." Ricoe got up and started pacing the floor out the blue. He couldn't even give her a straight face without turning to look the other way.

"It's all good because we can still cuddle and shit. We is together like that, a'ight. We got to start making real big moves soon. So, a good night's sleep will do us both some good. I know yo' ass is tied from moving that dough for our family and shit. One night off ain't going to kill our sex lives, right?" As soon as she said that her man was off to sleep. He didn't wait for her to get into bed or nothing. The only fucked up thing about it was that he had a big ass smile on his face. Ricoe had a nerve to be licking his lips too. Like a good girlfriend, Shabria started to undress her man to make him feel comfortable and shit. It was all good taking off his clothes to reveal his sexy, dark chocolate body. It looked so sweet and succulent that Shabria started to trail kisses all down his chest.

Shabria undid the belt buckle ready to taste and lick the goods. After his zipper slid down it was on. Shabria hungrily put all of him into her mouth. She devoured all of him with passionate sucking and licking. Getting all into it, she started to pull down his boxers and jeans to lick all over his moist pubic hair. For some reason, her man didn't get a hard on or wake the fuck up. Once his boxers and jeans dropped to his knees, an opened box fell out. *What is my fucking man doing with a box of Trojans in his jean pocket? It was fucking four rubbers in that bitch and now it's two? What fuck? Yo' nasty, cheating ass mutherfucker. Shabria, think for a minute. Fuck that, oh I got his ass alright.*

Shabria went straight to her kitchen to get a pot of ice-cold water. She ran the faucet water into the pot and was pissed. *Shit, this water ain't getting cold enough for that cheating dog.* Upset, she snatched the freezer door open to get the ice-trays. *I'm going to freeze that nigga's balls together! He'll learn tonight not to mess around on his woman!* Feeling accomplished with her cold concoction of freezing water and ice cubes, your girl was ready. The problem was that she filled the pot up too much. It was too for her to balance it without it tipping over and the fact that the handles were ice cold too. Between that and trying to tiptoe on the kitchen floor was bound to be a recipe for disaster. Shabria was trying not to wake her kids or her man up at that hour. It was already dark as shit because Shabria only had the stove light on. Trembling and the water shaking and splashing was all it took. Just like that, her crazy tail slipped and fell right on the hard kitchen floor. Not to mention, the entire pot of freezing water splattered all on her. Screaming out, her Prince Charming ran to her beck and call. As soon as that fool came, Shabria felt so stupid.

Ricoe came alright and with his phone in his hand. He had the camera facing her ready to record live and shit. He was standing there laughing like a crazed hyena. Shabria turned beet red and tried to get up but slipped back down instead.

Ricoe, yo' ass better not record me on this fucking kitchen floor. Turn that shit the fuck off!" Shabria yelled but he kept on laughing and recording.

"Men, this is one up for us! This is how you check the new chick for insecurities and this shit works every time. I, Ricoe Jones endorses this box of fine Trojan Condoms to fuck with yo' new girl and shit. We got to do what we got to do to reveal these crazy ass toxic chicks. We be in love with them, but damn. But to freeze our balls without hearing our side of the story first. Come on now guys admit that this is some scary, fucked up shit. Downright hilarious and truly uncalled for," said Ricoe while laughing and filming her live.

At first, Shabria was cussing on her knees while throwing paper cups and plastic knives at him. *This really is funny as shit. Look at us! I love being in love. I hope this crazy feeling lasts a lifetime.*

"Okay, okay! I get it. I just hate the fact that my boyfriend is a comedian, too. Yo' crazy, toxic ass cracks me up all day long. I'm sitting here in a puddle of ice water of you! I done wasted all my good paper cups and knives trying to kill you. I'm literally so over it," laughed Shabria. Ricoe grabbed a handful of paper towels to blot her dry while dying laughing.

"Wow, is that all you got for a Black King of yo' stature? No royal silk towels or a robe for yo' wet ass Queen. Where is your undying love and devotion for your fair lady?" asked crazy Shabria. It was too cute how Ricoe started tickling here while falling into the puddle with his love.

The way he took the edge of his shirt to wipe her face was breathtaking. Ricoe's hands were so gentle as he wiped her delicate face. They kissed like there was no tomorrow. Long succulent wet kisses with intertwining tongues. Shabria just melted in that mans eyes every time he touched her. Ricoe was putty in

his lover's embrace. Shabria's kisses took all his cares away. She made him feel like he was invincible and strong. Her love made him a better man. Ricoe had purpose, value and a life worth living because of Shabria. With her by his side there was no doubt that he could turn his life around for good. But with every victory there comes a resilience that we can not control. A dark side that lurks and preys on your transparency like a flesh-eating parasite. As much as Ricoe tried to do right it always resulted in bad things. His demons and spirits were imbedded into existence no matter how hard he tried to ger rid of them.

"I wish we could stay like this forever, Shabria. I know that I don't always show it. I don't even tell you how much I am in love with you half the time. You got my heart on a string, Girl and don't forget that. I would still be about that life if it wasn't for you, real talk. Because of you, I am a better man now. I can't say I'm perfect though. I'm trying, Bae. There are days and nights where I can't resist tapping back into my life before you. My past and its temptation still haunts my thoughts every minute. Yo' ass just don't know how hard it is for me. I know my silly ass like chopping it up and cracking jokes with you," said Ricoe sadly. Shabria put her arms around her man because she felt his pain. ***I can only imagine what my baby must have been through at some point in his life. Ricoe needs me in his life. From this day forth, it is going to me and him against the world, believe that. I got his back when he is down, 100%.***

"Baby, you and I got this! I didn't mean to add unnecessary pressure about no damn house. Shit, we can make it right here together if that's easier. Teamwork makes the dream work. I don't need no fucking salon right now, Black King. You got enough on yo' plate as it is. You took on a whole package deal

with me and my kids already. Let's put all that on the back burner. You is paying rent in two places and I feel bad about that, Baby. Why don't you just move in here with us? We can make it work. I know it. I done had the talk with the kids already about you moving in. It's all good, Baby. I am not with you for your cars and money, Ricoe. I just want yo' ass for real, real talk. I don't care if yo' ass lived in a cardboard box, I still would love you, unconditionally on gawd," cried Shabria. Ricoe wiped away her tears with his hands and he started crying instead.

That's what I needed to hear from my Queen. My girl has no idea of what my ass is into and that shit is going to stay that way. I respect my wifey so that what I do in the dark, her ass will never find out in the dark. I ain't come this fucking far to lose everything now. If wifey only knew the dirt I did and how much it costs me to keep it a secret from her. If I keep living a double life, I may have to move-in with her and her kids eventually. I hope it doesn't come to that point though because I love my freedom as a single man too much. Single as in un-married, **thought Ricoe to himself.**

"I am definitely working on it, my Queen. I am trying to figure out a way to break my lease as we speak. I can't wait to move in with my family. You have no idea how much that will mean to me! I can't wait to walk down that aisle and be gifted by God to have you as Mrs. Jones. Girl, you just don't know, do you? I ain't never leaving you and my kids, believe that!"

Out of the blue, Ricoe scooped his lover up in his arms like she was his prize. He carried her to their bed and ripped off her clothes as she lay on her back. He grabbed a jar of honey off the nightstand and poured it all over her naked body. That was all he wrote. He made the most passionate love to her mind and body. He lips explored every crease and opening on her body for hours.

When Shabria couldn't take it no more, he turned her on her stomach and told her to arch back on her knees. Shabria was so spent that she would do anything that he asked. Nothing was too forbidden or nasty when it came to her man pleasing her. Once the honey slid down her butt cheeks it was on. Ricoe dipped his fingers into her and then traced his juicy fingers around her lips. Shabria begged to taste her own juices but he said no and continued to tease her. He sniffed his own fingers clean and dry and continued to his main course. After he was done devouring his meal, her man jumped up like a thief in the night. Jiggling every sexy and delicious in the dark as he dashed to the bathroom.

In her mind, she wondered what was he up to now? He already done laid down the law and read her the rights. Shabria loved having a man that was full of sexual surprises in they bedroom. To this day, Shabria had never been made love to like that. Her man never seized to amaze her. It was like he could do no wrong. Her Ricoe was perfect in every way that counts. Shabria was caught up in a moment when she heard bathwater running in the top. The smell of ravishing red roses and lavender aromatherapy oils had awakened her senses. Ricoe was standing before her in the nude with a rose in his mouth. The fire and passion was still in his eyes like the day they first made love. Shabria crawled over to him and got on her knees. He moaned and cried out her name again and again.

After he loaded his children down her throat and dripped down her face, he spoke so seductively. "Come, my Queen! Let me wash away your fears and troubles. Let me drench my washcloth to take all yo' cares away like a man should and shit," said her man so seductively. Shabria was amazed at the twelve flickering scented candles all around their tub.

"My King, this is so amazing! What have I done in this lifetime to deserve all of this? This is the type of shit that I read about in fucking books for real! Who would have ever thought that ghetto ass Shabria Reid would live out such a fantasy," cried Shabria. Her heart told her to sing out cries of happiness and she did. Never in a million years, did she expect her man to sing along with her and in tune. They both were amazed because neither of them knew the other could sing like that. Like the old saying goes. "When you in love almost everything sounds good together but also note that everything that looks good usually isn't!"

"We sound good together, don't we, my Queen? Let's toast to Shabria and Ricoe forever, a'ight. These twelve red candles each represent my promise to you from this day forth. If I could, I would tell yo' red ass what they mean? Sorry wifey, but yo' king is still a little too intoxicated at the moment. I'm sure you get what I mean though. It's always the thought that counts," he cried with drunken tears.

Shabria ain't care because that shit sounded real good right about now. It may her want to let her guard down a little bit more and start trusting her man. Ricoe's word and undying love for her was golden.

Chapter 3: You get what you asked for!

A month later, everything went downhill. Her man did move the fuck in, but he had a lot of shit with his ass. Ricoe started going out every night and came creeping back in the wee hours of the morning. He went from late texting her back to not responding at all. To make matters worse, that fool's paper was running thin. It had got so bad that her ass had to beg for her one job back. Shabria remembered that fight like it was just yesterday. Ricoe's controlling ass had forbid her to work. Like a dummy, she obeyed his ass thinking that he was going to be their family's breadwinner and shit.

It was like Shabria had an adult son instead of a man. Shabria was tied of cleaning up behind his ass every night. Even the kid's was tied of Mr. Ricoe yelling at them for no reason. Ain't nothing or nobody made him happy no more. They constantly argued and fought about the stupidest things. Like not filling the ice tray up high enough. Not stacking the papercups up on the counter. *All his ass had to do was open up the fucking cupboards and get a damn cup. I'm going to be waiting for that ass at three am. Trust and believe that!*

Shabria was so happy that her kids had finished their dinner and had gone to they room. She just wanted to lay on her bed and cry her heart out. It clearly wasn't working out no more. Something or someone had changed her man and she could feel

it. Once again, it was times like these when she needed her two besties, Neicy and Trina. It would be over if she had to call that trifling mama of hers. The last timed they talked it didn't go to well. All she kept preaching about was that damn ninety day rule.

I'll be damned if that old gray haired woman wasn't telling the damn truth about our love thang. If my man cuts up one more time, me and the kids is definitely popping up unannounced. That crow obviously know something that my young ass don't for real.

Shabria must have cried herself to sleep because it was damn near seven am. Shabria rolled over expecting to bump into her man. Boy, was she in for a surprise. Her dumb ass kept right on rolling until she fell of the bed. Hitting the floor seems different when yo' ass realize you is getting the fuck played.

Shabria looked around her room and there were no signs of him ever coming home. She hollered for the kids to take a shower and get dressed immediately. Shabria shook her head thinking how they each had to get dressed in that steamy cramped place, too. It ain't like they had separate bedrooms, so the kids had to do what they had to do for real. The worse part about that was when Tyrik's fat ass had too much applesauce. It gave him diarrhea real bad. Every second his ass would bang on the bathroom door because he had to take a shit. It was gross and stinky as fuck too. Ti'aja would blame her mother for keeping buying that mess in the first place. "Ma, we is running out of toilet paper and spray as it is. Buy his fat tail bananas for that loose stool instead," Ti'aja whined. It was true but Shabria ain't want to take all his favorite things away. Now that Ricoe was there it was harder for him to act his age as it was. Ricoe was always hollering at him and telling him to fix things around the house.

Tighten up the chair legs. Plunge the toilet since yo' ass done stopped it up. Now that one, Shabria agreed with. All his lying ass did was preach about his life growing up in some damn West Baltimore and shit.

Fabricating the story as he went along for clout. I was the man of the house at six-years-old. *Yeah right, Ricoe. Fast forward to today fool. I had to change my own tire because yo' ass was too intoxicated to think straight. While I'm at it. Our bedroom doorknob is loose from yo' ass keep slamming it. Our headboard is still loose. I can go on and on but it ain't worth it for real, you feel me!* Just saying shit out loud must do something for his Pinocchio lying ass. My granny ain't need nothing fixed by no maintenance man. Shit, I did it for free, a'ight. I was man back then and still is to this day.*All fucking lies. His ass just likes to hear himself talk and shit,* thought Shabria to herself.

Shabria hopped in the shower after Tyrik. Her cramps was something fierce. It was a good thing to see some blood because she ain't need to be pregnant on top of everything else going wrong in her life. Her period was a whole two weeks late as it was. In about an hour, they all was dressed in ready to ride in her hoopdy once again. *To grandma's house, we go. If I wasn't so desperate, I would have never come to this old owl for no advice. I know that for a fact being old don't make yo' ass wise. Mama Tawanda was just nosey as hell. Always minding other people's affairs and shit. Tawanda's old self ain't never practice what she preached in her own hot messes. With Trina and Neicy out my life, who is I'm supposed to turn to, for real? I should know better than to tell her gossiping ass any fucking thing of importance. I got to be one desperate, stupid son of a gun for that one! My mama just going to tweet my mess on Twitter and shit. At her age, she still be posting everybody's else's business for fame and clout. I mean, come on now. At forty-six-years old why is her ass still impressed by getting likes and follows?*

That ass is too old to be an insta-hoe on the gram. Ain't no grandma that age should be TikToking and Snap Chatting. Like really, Ma! At the end of the day, a girl is always going to need they mama no matter what.

The drive to her mama's wasn't that bad. Tawanda lived right over Belair-Edison. It was decent over there. Her mama ain't have any problems that she knew of. Mama lived in a nice lil' two bedroom duplex. That work because it was just her. Onve upon a time, Shabria considered moving there with her young kids when Tyrik's dumb ass got locked up. His lying ass swore down that he had paid they rent up for six months. That worked because her and her mama ain't always been on the best of terms anyway. It only took two days for they landlord to post a yellow eviction notice on the apartment though. Shabria figured she must have heard her baby daddy wrong because that ass was actually six months behind and shit. It took three minimum wage jobs and giving old Landlord Fred some coochie to stay there until she got caught up. *Fred, was a disgusting old man that preyed on his most vulnerable tenants, government assisted single mothers. He used they situation to get some knowing damn well he ain't miss no forty-dolla rent. Section eight paid that fool faithfully every first of the month. Thinking back, they probably weren't even real eviction notices!*

Going up her sidewalk, you could smell the burning incense. That was another reason she ain't want her babies to stay there. That secondhand smoke wasn't no joke for real. Mama Tawanda was addicted to them stinking sticks like crazy. For the life of her, she wondered why her mama ain't go to the Dollar Store right up the street instead. Her crazy self ain't believe in no mushroom air fresheners or oil plug-ins like most normal people did, me included.

Her mama was in the kitchen as usual smoking a blunt and scratching a pile of scratch-offs. *Why, who knows because she don't ever win nothing.*

"Uhm, Sista Girl! I'm going to be needing my spare house key back. Y'all can't be doing no surprise pop ups and shit. Sometimes, I like to walk around my house bucket naked," laughed Tawanda.

"Y'all adults is so nasty, Granny. That's what Mr. Ricoe does at our place. Granny he done moved in and everything," snitched Ti'aja. Shabria ain't never felt so embarrassed in her life. She was seconds away from smacking the beads right out of her plaits. Looking like a mini me, Bo Derek and shit.

"Tyrik and Ti'aja, kiss y'all Grandma and go outside and play before I catch a charge today." They kissed and hugged Tawanda followed by light chit chat. Shabria gave them the eye like they better watch what the fuck they say. After something to drink and eat real quick, they lil' asses bounced.

"Look what the cat done dragged back in! Yo' new man is cheating on that high yella ass or yo' ass is pregnant, Shabria. Being that it a ripe old ninety-day mark, yo' dumb ass is probably both. Don't say I ain't warn yo' dumb ass now. Let me guess Ricoe is fucking Neicy, Trina or both of them right. Now, yo' ass done came crying back to mama to see what to do, right?" snapped Tawanda. Shabria did one of Ricoe's numbers and started pacing the floor. She tried to avoid eye contact as long as she could too. The mama has spoken.

"Fuck them, let them have the man temporarily Shabria. It's only lust and infatuation. Any man with the right head on they shoulders will get tied of community cooch. Especially, Neicy's nasty ass. Ain't no man with good sense going to turn that hoe into no girlfriend, Shabria," yelled Tawanda.

Shabria had to sit down on that one. Mama's tea was boiling hot and spilling the truth even if she ain't want to hear that shit out loud.

"Maybe, that thot Neicy. Definitely not Trina, her ass to wholesome. Up to this day, her ass is still a fucking virgin even with a new man on her arms. Sis, ain't nasty enough to get and keep anybody's man for real," said Shabria trying to convince herself of that lie. *I hate when that goat looks all simple and shakes her head like that.*

"Trina, possibly because she's his type. I know that because I asked my man, Ma. Trina, I disagree. Yo' ass needs to lay off that weed because I thought you said to let her keep my man! Mama, you must have lost yo' everlasting mind. You is telling me to share him!" yelled Shabria.

"I know yo' ass heard that saying that besties share everything right because they do. If I was in they situation I would have done the same. Shit, if I was fit and twenty- years younger even I would have fucked the shit out that fine ass chocolate man myself. At least, I'm keeping it real. Every woman should know that a jealous bitch will try to fuck they man when a opportunity presents himself. His fine ass work, drive and got his own shit too. Come on now, stop acting so fucking simple and childish about the damn man, Shabria. To let the shit hit the fan. His cheating is yo' fault. Yes, I said it and what?" snapped crazy Tawanda.

"Ma, just say no to drugs because yo' ass is talking out the side of yo' chicken neck for real. I'm taking care of my man's needs in the bedroom, thank-you! You ain't saying nothing for real," yelled Shabria. *I'll be dammed if I let her trifling ass see me cry.*

How she going to school me on my man when she ain't got one herself? That Rose Toy can never take the place of a mouth. I should have never came the fuck over here like a dumb fool for real.

"I ain't got to be on drugs to know that all men want that tight, untouched cooch of Trina's. That nasty Neicy is a feisty ratchet chick. The type them hood thugs go for. So, I know one of them is fucking yo' man based on simple Science, Shabria. Neither of them got baggage and they both is chocolate pretty girls who is easy on the eye. Being fucking red ain't enough to keep a fine brutha like that. Stop being childish, selfish and conceited all yo' life. Run that man's bath water and drank it from time to time. Cook him homecooked meals, child. Wash them dirty ass clothes and feet, too. Make his ass feel appreciated and needed. Yo' dumb ass probably done told him it ain't all about no money. Yo' dumb ass has always been a dizzy bitch, Girl. If yo' ass ain't collecting his money one of them damn sure is. You put your foot in yo' own mouth on that one. I'm still scratching my head trying to figure out how I even birthed a high-yella baby like you for real," shouted Tawanda and she had a nerve to hug her like it's all good.

"Take care of yo' home before you worry about the next bitch. Her place is temporary, a'ight! Yo' ass got his heart and that will last a lifetime, baby girl. He will get tied and come back to you if you ass is willing and ready. You already done got one up over them, her or whatever. Ricoe, lives with you and accepts yo' kids as his own. Just think on yo' own for once and you can have yo' man back. I been in both positions so I know the deal. It obvious that y'all love each other. Don't be a fool and loose him to that bitch, Neicy. Remember, you had him first, a'ight," said her Mama sincerely this time.

Her mama even agreed to watch her kids for a few days and shit. Tawanda knew somebody that knew somebody with a timeshare and shit. A nice little cabin in the mountains for real. That gave her hope and motivation. Although he stayed out all the time and barely came home, Shabria was chill about it. She googled how to keep a man and what makes a man cheat. Ricoe was definitely the apple of her eye so it was all good.

Shabria started cooking at home and it ain't work at first. Eventually, Ricoe got tired of the greasy chicken boxes and steak subs. Shabria used her free time to work out and shit. Surprisingly, Mama Tawanda offered to babysit Tyrik and Ti'aja more. Shabria did ask Ricoe for money to buy sexy lingerie and sex toys for their bedroom. Although she ain't feel all that sexy with a lil' bulge forming in her stomach. Her period still was late as hell. Shabria bought a pregnancy test to take with them on their romantic getaway and shit.

After begging him and begging him, Ricoe agreed to go. His ass did get tied of the city life and the thots in it. The weeks leading up to the trip, he did stick around their apartment more. He still got late night texts and his phone stayed powered off. A few times while dropping off her kids, Tawanda hinted at her picking up some healthy weight finally.

Shabria had to admit that things were slowly getting better between them. It took a while but at least they were finally in a good place again. Shabria was a lil' hesitant about doing his

favorite sex positions out of fear of an impending, yet very possible early pregnancy.

One morning though, Shabria was dying to know if she was having her man's baby or not. Shabria ran to the corner store to get an early pregnancy test. She read online that the first morning urine had the highest HCG. Her three minutes was up...........